DIAMONDS

OTHER TITLES BY K.A. LINDE

AVOIDING SERIES

Avoiding Commitment (#1)
Avoiding Responsibility (#2)
Avoiding Intimacy (#2.5)
Avoiding Decisions (#1.5)
Avoiding Temptation (#3)

RECORD SERIES

Off the Record
On the Record
For the Record

TAKE ME DUET

Take Me for Granted
Take Me with You

Following Me

DIAMONDS

USA *Today* Bestselling Author
k.a. linde

Diamonds, All That Glitters

By K.A. Linde

Copyright © 2015 by K.A. Linde

All rights reserved.

Cover Designer: Sarah Hansen, Okay Creations, www.okaycreations.com

Editor and Interior Designer: Jovana Shirley, Unforeseen Editing, www.unforeseenediting.com

Poem reprinted with permission © r.m. drake, instagram.com/rmdrk

Visit my website at http://www.kalinde.com

ISBN-13: 9781682308684

listen, i am not someone who
is easy to love. i am not
someone who is to be taken lightly
and most of all, i am not someone
to burn.

for i am the fire, my soul is on
fire and everything i live to
touch becomes one with the fire.

—r.m. drake

ONE

BROKEN—mind, body, and soul.

Begging to forget her meaningless existence, to be commanded and molded and remade into someone else, she needed the embrace of the nightlife, the pounding of the music, the sweat, the intoxication just to *feel* again.

If even for one night.

Allure wasn't Bryna's usual scene. She preferred exclusive nightclubs in Beverly Hills and house parties that catered to her and her überwealthy friends at Harmony Prep. She favored places where everyone knew her name, and she could rule as queen bee. But, tonight, she didn't want to rule her throne.

She wanted to forget her own reality and get lost in the imagined one that Allure provided. The room was full to the brim with bodies grinding to the music and people drinking top-shelf liquor and indulging in the dark secret desires of their hearts.

She swirled the gin martini in her hand and pursed her lips as she surveyed the room.

It was easier here.

Easier to forget about her Hollywood parents and their pathetic divorce. Easier to forget that her high-profile director father had remarried this summer to some Valley trash he'd been having an affair with while he was with her mom. Easier to forget that she had three new stepsiblings and that the oldest, Pace, was only a year younger than her and the new starting quarterback at school.

Easier to forget about everything.

At least everything that was cluttering up her picture-perfect life. Despite the heinous drama consuming her, she needed to remember who she was and what she stood for.

She was fucking *Bryna Turner*.

A goddess at Harmony. Queen bee. Head cheerleader.

She had started dating Gates Hartman before his breakout role, and now, he was the hottest up-and-coming actor who had hit Hollywood since Ryan Gosling.

She refused to give two shits about what anyone thought of her, especially her parents. Her world might have shifted with the upheaval of their marriage, but she had remained strong for all the eyes always watching her.

But tonight was different.

Tonight, no one was watching.

Tonight, she could lose herself, lose control.

And maybe that was what brought him closer.

TWO

"SCOTCH NEAT."

The bartender nodded at the man standing next to Bryna at the bar and grabbed the top-shelf liquor.

Perfect.

Bryna tipped back the last of her martini and set it down on the counter. She licked her lips. "One more for me."

The man turned to take her in. His eyes snagged on her slinky royal-blue dress, her chest popping out of the deep scoop neck. Then he looked up into her baby-blue eyes. He grinned. "Put that on my tab."

She met his gaze and arched an eyebrow. "Thanks."

"I've never seen you here before," he said a moment later.

"Maybe you weren't looking hard enough."

Oh, he likes that.

He angled his tall muscular body toward her. His hair was dark as night, cut short and styled like a European soccer player. His eyes were milk chocolate and danced in the dim light. "I'm glad I've found you now."

A smile stretched across her face. She couldn't disagree with him.

He splayed his hand out on the bar to reach for the scotch resting before him, and her stomach dropped.

Third finger on the left hand.

Silver band.

Married.

It might as well have been a brand on his skin. It was screaming at her to walk away.

No. Don't walk.

Run. Run far away from this.

Bad, bad idea.

She dropped the seductive smile from her face. As soon as the martini was set in front of her, she took the drink and backed away. She wouldn't do that. Even flirting with him made her skin crawl. She liked bad ideas, but she had lines she wouldn't cross. Her parents' marriage had been torn apart by this very thing. Her stepmother, Celia, had destroyed everything sacred, walked across every line, and forced Bryna's father to leave her mother.

Vows were supposed to mean something, and Celia hadn't cared about them. Bryna barely saw her father now as he was always out working on-site. Instead of moving out with her mother, she had stayed in his house with that wretched woman because of Harmony. She only had one year left.

4

Leaving now and starting over at some other school would be impossible.

"Are you all right?" he asked, lightly placing his right hand on her slim shoulder.

She recoiled from his touch. *How dare he!*

"You're married," she spat.

"Oh."

He looked down at his hand, and his face fell. The sadness in his eyes was all-encompassing before he recovered and locked everything away inside of him. She only recognized the reaction because she had been doing it every day for the last year as her whole world had split apart, leaving her in perpetual free fall.

"I'm...we're separated." He slid the ring from his finger and held it out in front of him. "Honestly, I forgot I had it on."

She pursed her lips. She didn't want him to bullshit her. *Who forgets they are wearing a goddamn wedding ring?*

"You don't believe me," he said, taking in her appearance. He tucked the ring into his pocket, out of sight.

"My tolerance for married men is very low."

He smirked. "Daddy issues?"

"Like you'd never believe."

"Let me guess. He left her for a younger woman."

"Bingo."

"Well, I'm not in that situation."

She shook her head. "Nor will I be, which is why I have to say good-bye."

"Stay."

Her eyes met his, and he wasn't exactly pleading with her. It was more of a command, more of a desire to get to know her, to find out what was making her run so easily.

"I won't be made a fool of," she told him.

"I know."

"You're not with her?"

"No," he answered immediately.

She narrowed her eyes, and he knowingly met her gaze. No hidden agenda. Just a mirror of the emotions skittering through her.

"Fine." She snapped her fingers at the bartender. "Tequila shots, please." She held up two fingers.

The bartender poured the shots for them, and they knocked them back. The liquid burned down her throat, but she ignored the pain as she sucked on the lime. His eyes traveled to her lips. She purposely licked the juice off her finger. Her tongue swirled her thumb, and he watched her with utter fascination and longing.

He possessed none of the idiocy of the guys she had dated before, not even Gates. The person in front of her was a *man*. And completely delectable. At the youngest, he was in his late twenties. No less than ten years older than her seventeen years.

Even before he ever made the first move, she knew that he knew what he was doing to her with that look.

THREE

"SO, WHAT ABOUT YOU?"

"What about me?" Bryna asked.

"Well, you can't possibly be single."

She laughed lightly and ducked her chin to her chest. No, of course she wasn't single. But as far as she knew, Gates didn't care if she flirted with every guy in Hollywood as long as she was on his arm when he needed her. They had known each other a long time, and he liked that he didn't have to explain himself to her, let alone have her fawn over him for doing something he had always been naturally good at. She treated him exactly the same way she did everyone else, and their relationship had blossomed naturally out of their mutual understanding.

"You say that with such surety," she said.

He tucked a lock of her blonde hair behind her ear. "You are the most exquisite thing I've ever seen. I'm sure you have people knocking your door down."

"Yet I'm here all alone."

"Waiting for someone?" he guessed.

She shook her head.

"Anyone going to break down my door when we leave?"

Damn. He was so sure of himself. She liked the self-confidence he wore like a cloak. It was her biggest turn-on.

Gates had it in spades, but it was nothing compared to this guy. And it wasn't as if Gates would be busting down anyone's door to get to her. He was on set on the East Coast, filming his new movie, *Broken Road.* She hadn't seen him in months, not since she had flown out there this summer.

And she wasn't even sure Gates would be angry. She could probably tell him tomorrow that she had fucked this guy, and she doubted she would see an ounce of fury. Maybe some wounded pride. Maybe a touch of jealousy over someone touching what belonged to him. But he wouldn't really be angry.

Their relationship had never been like that. Sometimes, she thought she was just more of a convenience for him.

Her silence spurred the man forward.

"Ah, so there is someone."

She shrugged and averted her baby-blue eyes.

"An idiot to leave you here all alone," he continued.

"Why? He's a very secure man. I doubt he'd think anyone could come in an sweep me off my feet."

"Then, he truly is an idiot," he said in a heartbeat.

He stepped toward her, and she had to tilt her head up to look at him.

But she didn't move away or back down. She could play along. "You don't know him."

"Should I?"

She bit her lip. She didn't want him to know who she was. If she told him she was dating Gates Hartman, well, then that would be the end of their game. And she really liked playing this game.

"No," she finally said. "I don't think you should."

"Good."

His hand slid around her waist where his long fingers splayed across her lower back. Her heart thrummed to a beat from his touch. She was warm everywhere at once. If he kept this fire simmering in her core, she knew there would be no going back.

She held on to her confidence and met his dark gaze. The gaze of the devil incarnate tempting her to sin, offering her the apple from the Garden of Eden. Perhaps he was a snake. But if sin tasted this good, then she understood why Eve had thirsted for knowledge.

"Dance?" he suggested.

His hand slid into hers and drew her out to the dance floor. They were soon consumed by people and lost in the crowd. He pressed her back into his chest. Their hips swayed to the beat. His fingers dug into the material of her tight dress, and she groaned at the feel of him. He knew exactly what he was doing.

The heat between them escalated. He pulled her hands over her head and around his neck. He pressed his pelvis into her ass as she ground herself against him. His mouth touched the sensitive skin on her neck, and she shivered all over. He traveled up to her ear, and then grasped her chin, forcing her to give him better access. His lips settled along her jaw and then her cheek. Her eyes fluttered closed in the dark room. Her skin vibrated under his touch as she anticipated what was to come. She swallowed, barely breathing, as she felt the gentlest of brushes. A taste. A test.

Then, he was kissing her. The world went dark. The kiss was hot and insistent and as greedy as the music moving through the bodies around them.

His tongue brushed against her lips, and she opened her mouth to let him in. Their tongues met, and she was lost. She voraciously pulled his mouth down onto hers, never wanting to break away.

As the kiss intensified, he turned her around and drew her into his arms. Her body was on fire. Her face was flushed. Her hands clutched the collar of his shirt. She could do this all night.

She broke away, breathless. Her pupils blasted out, and her chest heaved.

Their game was coming to an end. She had forfeited the prize in the heat of the moment on the crowded dance floor.

"Leave with me," he breathed into her ear.

"How do I know I can trust you?"

He lightly nipped her ear, and she shivered.

"You don't."

FOUR

THE INCLINATION TO LEAVE WITH HIM ate at her like a virus infecting her body. She had been with older men before—not quite as old as him, usually college guys—so it wasn't just the taboo factor that infatuated her.

It was something about *him*.

She didn't know his name, where he was from, what he did. She didn't know *anything*. Just that he was married. Separated. She gathered he was wealthy by the fact that he was at this club, wearing an expensive suit, and drinking top-shelf scotch. All these things mattered in her world even if her dad had chosen to ignore them by marrying beneath him.

But what intrigued her the most was precisely that she didn't know if she could trust him. Yet, without that knowledge, maybe because of the danger and mystery, she still wanted to leave with him.

She was sure it was more than just the fact that she wanted to fuck him. It was something in his eyes that said he understood her. It was something in his smile that said he identified with what she was going through. It was something in his confidence that said he recognized the act she was putting on. It was something about the desire in that kiss that said he would *worship* her.

Fuck caution.

"Let's go," she said finally.

He smiled smugly as if he always knew things would end this way. Perhaps he had. She hadn't exactly made it difficult for him. She could have, but she was sure he still would have fought for her.

"I'll close out my tab," he told her.

He took her hand and guided her back to the bar.

While he had his back to her, she fished her phone out of her clutch and pulled up Gates's number. She hit Call and waited. He answered at the last second in a drowsy haze. She hadn't even considered that she was three hours behind him. The time difference always fucked with his sleep schedule.

"Babe," he murmured in greeting.

"It's over, Gates."

"Hmm?" He yawned on the other line. "Tonight?"

"No. Forever."

"What's going on?" He seemed to be growing more alert.

"I'm breaking it off."

"You with someone else?"

He didn't even sound hurt, just curious. She had suspected as much, but it irritated her more than she had thought.

"Yeah."

"All right. I'll see you when I get back to L.A."

"No," she said, frustrated. "This is really over."

He chuckled softly into the phone. "Bri, you want other dick. That's fine."

"*Why* is that fine?"

Gates always brought out the more human side of her that she usually hid behind her hard exterior.

"Because I'm on the other side of the country and not able to give you what you need. When I come back, we'll figure it out."

She shook her head. *Why does he have to take this so calmly?*

Fucking asshole.

"We're not going to figure it out. I don't think I should have to dumb it down for you to understand what I'm telling you. I said, it's over. I mean, it's over. Good night, Gates."

She hung up the phone before he could say another word. *Well, that was an interesting conversation.* Of all the things she had expected from Gates, she hadn't wagered for disbelief. She was Bryna Turner. She could get any guy she wanted. *How could he not believe that I would find someone else? Is he that conceited?*

By the time he realized that she was serious, she would be long gone.

"Ready to go?" the man asked, coming up behind her.

"Yes."

"Good."

He didn't ask about her conversation, and she was glad. She didn't want to tell him about it.

"Lead the way," she told him.

Grabbing her hand, he walked her through the crowded bar and out onto the street. He passed his ticket to the valet. A few minutes later, a shiny Jaguar convertible pulled up in front of Allure.

She raised her eyebrows in appreciation. Her father collected cars, so she had been taught to drive a stick as soon as her feet could reach the pedals. She wouldn't mind taking this beauty out for a joyride. Her eyes traveled back to the man who was climbing into the driver's side. Maybe a joyride of a different nature.

"Nice ride," she said. "XKR-S, next year's model. This thing goes zero to sixty in about four seconds and has a top speed of, what? One eighty? Two hundred?"

"One eighty-six." He looked over at her, impressed. "You know cars?"

"I know a thing or two," she said, running her hand down the side of the car. She sank into the passenger seat and glanced over at him in wonder. "So, what do you do?"

He winced slightly and gave her an apologetic look.

Oh.

So, it's like that? I'm not supposed to know any personal details about him?

That's fine.

Whatever.

"Never mind," she muttered. *I'm not that kind of girl. Fuck!*

"Sorry. The last woman who asked me that was a gold digger."

He did look like he was sorry. But he had just compared her to a fucking gold digger.

"And do you think *I'm* a gold digger just because I asked you about your job?"

He shrugged. "You can never be too careful."

She glared at him. If she was going to share information about herself, then she could dress him down with how ludicrous it was to call *her* a gold digger. Her father was a multimillion-dollar director, her mother was an actress, and even her grandmother had been a successful actress. *She* would never need to stoop to such degrading extremes for money. She lived in Bel Air and went to school in Beverly Hills.

Enough said.

"I'm not a fucking gold digger. I just like your car."

"Okay."

"And anyway you wouldn't be driving it if you didn't want people to admire it."

He shrugged. "Fair enough."

The drive to his place didn't take as long as she had anticipated. With him driving a car like this, she had expected him to be in a gated community in the Hills. She knew the area they were in though. It was full of wealthy apartments and condominiums for people who worked in the city and didn't want to deal with traffic. Her father preferred to stay at a suite at the Beverly Wilshire, or the like, when he had business in the city, but he had colleagues who would get similar apartments.

They took the elevator to the top floor and walked into a large suite apartment. It was immaculately decorated but didn't have a scrap of personal touch to it. No pictures of the wife he was separated from. Nothing to suggest he was anything but an affluent businessman.

"Drink?" he offered.

"How about a name?"

He sent her a curious look and then walked toward a bar on the other side of the room. He poured two glasses of scotch from a crystal decanter and brought one over to her. She weighed it in her hands and nearly smiled in delight at the quality.

"Have you ever done this before?"

She stared straight ahead. "Done what?"

He came up behind her and spoke softly into her ear, "Been with a stranger."

She shivered. "Yes."

It was kind of the truth. She had fooled around with guys she had met only a handful of times at parties, but she had never allowed them to go further than that.

"I like the mystery of not knowing." He trailed his hand down her arm.

She had to do everything not to shiver all over again. "So...you do this often?" She didn't keep the bite out of her voice. He laughed melodically behind her and nipped at her neck. "Is this why you're separated?"

He sighed. "No. That's...complicated." He clearly didn't want to talk about it. "But to answer your first question, I don't do this often. And I've certainly never met anyone as beautiful as you."

"Flattery doesn't work," she said.

"Oh?" His hand trailed down the gold zipper of her form-fitting dress. He stopped right before it reached her ass and then splayed his hand out across her lower back. "It's hardly flattery when it's the truth."

"A name."

"Any name?"

She turned around to face him and stared up into his intense dark eyes. *What secrets is he hiding? Could it possibly be as many as I am keeping?*

She felt it in the pit of her stomach that somehow he felt as empty as she did. She walked through life, surrounded by a sea of blindingly happy people. Life had been laid out before them, and they didn't have a care in the world.

But when she looked up at him, the emptiness that had consumed her after her parents' divorce, maybe even before that, seemed to find a twin.

"Just a name. It can't be that hard." She breathed out slowly in anticipation. "I'm Bri."

With the nickname, she could at least keep him from figuring out that she was Bryna Turner. There weren't many Brynas in Hollywood, even fewer pronounced *Brihn-uh*. She wasn't ready for him to know that name, not when it could lead him back to the fact that she was in high school.

He mulled over the name for a second before sticking his hand out and responding, "Jude."

FIVE

"WHAT'S GOING ON in that pretty little head of yours?" He took a drink of his scotch. His eyes stared straight through her.

"Just admiring your taste in scotch."

Bryna distracted herself from that stare by taking a sip of her drink. Single malt, undeniably smooth, and utterly delicious. She did *not* need this to feel more confident. She was *not* nervous. In fact, she wanted this.

She was Bryna Turner. Nothing could break her stride.

His lips quirked up. "You know one of the first things I noticed about you?"

"My tits?" she joked, deflecting.

His eyes flicked down to her exposed cleavage and then back up. "After I saw how beautiful you were."

"What?" She was intrigued.

"How truly empty you looked."

In shock, Bryna faltered backward a step. She didn't care that his words exactly mirrored what she thought about him every time she looked into his eyes. It didn't matter that she truly did feel empty or that her parents' divorce had rendered her this way. *How could he say that to my face?*

"I am *not* empty," she spat.

"I'm sure that's what you tell everyone." He set his glass down on the coffee table and came back around to stand behind her. "You hide behind a wall of self-confidence. No one can see past the hardened exterior."

She felt the faint brush of his hand along her shoulder and up her neck.

"But I do. I see what you keep hidden, what you want no one else to see."

"I have no idea what you're talking about. This is who I am."

Jude's mouth replaced his hand, and suddenly, it took everything in her not to lean back into that kiss. Chills ran up her arms. The anticipation of what was to come increased her sensitivity to his touch. Every brush, every touch of his lips sent a shock wave through her system.

"This body," he murmured, running his hands down her sides and over her hips, "hides how hollow you are on the inside."

He dug his fingers into her hips, and she struggled to remember how to respond.

"I…no."

"Something stripped you down and left your soul bare." His hand slid to her thigh and under the hem of her dress. "As bare as you're about to be."

"Jude," she whispered. She didn't know what else to say. She wanted to argue. *But really, what's the point? How can he see what no one else has been able to?*

"You know I'm right." He roughly turned her around and looked deeply into her eyes.

His fingers twined in her hair, and she closed her eyes as he tilted her head up toward him.

"Tell me I'm right."

Trying to keep her walls up around him was futile. Everywhere else, she had to pretend that she was whole and fine, that nothing could bring her down, nothing could hurt. If the opportunity to be herself and to be with someone who understood her pain was presenting itself to her, then she was going to take it.

"You're right."

He didn't ask her to talk about it or explain the feelings behind her emptiness. And she didn't ask him to try to make it better. A mutual understanding bloomed between them, something no one else could touch. In that moment, she knew she was lost.

His lips crashed down on top of hers, forceful and demanding. He was in charge. He took control. It was clear he knew exactly what he was doing.

Her scotch glass disappeared from her hand, and then he guided her back to his bedroom. The glass balcony doors, covered in sheer curtains, let in a dim glow of light. A king-sized bed took up the center of the room with a black leather bed frame, a charcoal bedspread, and black throw pillows. It was dark and exotic.

Jude's lips melted with hers for a minute, tasting and testing. When he pulled back, she was left wanting more. She didn't feel as hollow with his lips on hers.

"Stand right here," he instructed, positioning her to face the bed.

She curiously looked at him as he sat down in front of her. She wanted to make some comment about how she could have just *stood* at the bar, but she held her tongue. She was confident in her skin. She didn't mind him examining her from head to toe.

And he did just that.

"Now, take off your dress. Slowly."

She arched an eyebrow, and he just smirked back in return with a challenge glinting in his eyes. She could play this game if that was what he wanted even if it would be her first real striptease.

Turning to face away from him, she spread her legs more than shoulder width apart, stretching the elastic material until the dress rode up her legs. Then, she reached for the zipper on the back and very carefully dragged it down. First, she revealed the royal-blue La Perla bra, then the matching lace panties, and finally the curve of her ass. She dropped the dress off of each shoulder and then gingerly pushed it over her hips where it pooled at her feet.

She heard his intake of breath, and it encouraged her to continue.

She slowly walked in a small half circle to face him in nothing but her lingerie and Louboutins. Red lacquered heels were her specialty.

"Proof that your dress looks better on my floor."

Bryna walked forward, one foot in front of the other, swaying seductively. She pushed him backward on the bed, climbed on top of him, and threaded his tie through her fingers. "So will your suit."

"I'm going to fuck you in those heels." He rolled her over on the bed and started stripping out of his suit. "Just those heels."

"You'll have to do something about this lingerie."

"I don't care if I have to rip it off," he said as his pants fell to the floor, leaving him in nothing but his black boxer briefs.

His body covered hers a second later, reaching under her body until he unclasped her bra. He pulled it over her head and watched as her glorious breasts fell into place.

"Fuck," he muttered. His hands caressed them, stiffening her nipples, and then he sucked on the hardened points.

She arched her back and wound her fingers through his hair. He hadn't moved an inch lower, and her blood was pounding. She was already wet and close to soaking through the thin material keeping him from her. She tilted her hips up hoping to encourage him to move farther south, but he only laughed at her.

"Not yet," he murmured softly.

Then, out of nowhere, his tie reappeared. He had her hands clasped above her head, and he was tying the material around her wrists. The tie wasn't attached to anything, but his point was clear.

Don't move.

Her heart rate skyrocketed. He had tied her hands together. *Shit!*

He went back to work on her tits. He alternated between giving her pain and pleasure as he nipped at the sensitive peaks and rolled them between his fingers. She felt ready to combust under the attention and all before he even yanked her underwear to the ground to find out exactly how wet she already was.

One finger went in, and he groaned. She had to resist bucking off the bed as a second followed, and then he was working her in and out. Slowly at first, and then he picked up the pace as he brought her closer to climax. Her eyes were closed, and she was digging her fingers into the comforter when she felt his tongue flick against her clit. Her body jerked. Then, he was giving it the same treatment as her nipples. He swirled his tongue around the nub and licked and sucked until she was convulsing underneath him.

She was in ecstasy from her orgasm when she felt his dick pressed against her opening. Her body tightened around the head, and she pushed her hips toward him.

"Fucking hell," he groaned.

He withdrew from within her, and her eyes snapped open, full of questions. She saw him tear open a condom, and she nearly groaned herself. She would have rather felt him against her, inside her.

But she didn't protest, and then he plunged deep into her. She cried out as he filled her. For once, she didn't feel empty or hollow. She felt completely and totally full. Of his cock.

He leaned forward, so one of his hands rested on her bound wrists, and then he started working her back into a frenzy. He pulled out slow and then slammed into her as fast as he could. Over and over and every agonizing moment over again, he would thrust into her until she was shaking with the need for release, but then he would be deliberately gentle and hold her off for another minute.

His lips fell hungrily on hers, and she felt him somehow expanding further inside her. He was as close as she was. They were both ready to collapse from exhaustion and the pent-up energy.

"Do you want to come, beautiful?"

She nodded her head. *How am I even holding on to composure?* All she wanted was for him to make her explode.

His hands fell to the sides of her face, and they passionately locked lips once more as he thrust into her until they both let go. Bryna's body shook from head to toe. She threw her head back as waves of heat passed through her. She saw stars in her vision.

When it finally cleared, she looked up at the man who had taken her to all new heights. She knew there was no going back from here.

SIX

THE NEXT MORNING, Bryna awoke to an empty bed. She sat up, clutching the bedsheet to her chest, and looked around the dark room.

No Jude.

She scooted off the bed and winced as she stood. Her body reminded her exactly how much physical exertion it had endured last night. She shimmied back into her dress, grabbed her shoes, and walked out into the living room.

"Jude," she called out.

No response.

She ducked her head into the guest bedroom and the kitchen, looked into both bathrooms, and even decided to peer into the closets.

Empty.

What the fuck?

They'd had an incredible connection and an even more incredible night. Then, he had ditched her?

What kind of scumbag would do that to me? Has he been playing games the whole time? Have I been a conquest?

She was *not* just some conquest!

She quickly made arrangements for a cab to come pick her up and then stormed to the door. On her way out, she noticed a piece of paper on a table next to the exit. She snatched it into her hand.

I GOT CALLED INTO WORK AND DIDN'T WANT TO WAKE YOU. STAY AS LONG AS YOU LIKE, BUT I DON'T KNOW WHEN I'LL GET BACK TO THE APARTMENT. SORRY TO RUN OUT ON YOU.

—JUDE

Contemplating, Bryna rolled the paper over in her hand. This could be the truth. She didn't know what line of work he was in, but her father worked most Saturdays. It was a reasonable assumption that he worked a lot to have amassed such a fortune.

She ground her teeth. She didn't want to think it was okay for him not to even say good-bye. But he had left a note. Well, if it were all true, then he would get in touch with her again. She scribbled down her number on the bottom of the paper and signed it *Bri.*

She was sure she would hear from him soon enough.

After leaving Jude's apartment, the cab took forever to get back to her dad's place. She had to be at school soon for the away football game tonight. It was weird even thinking about going back to high school after being with Jude.

Her life felt upside down and inside out. There was the most fulfilling night of her life, where she had been completely free, and then there was the rest of the world. If Jude hadn't more or less left her high and dry, she wouldn't have ever wanted to come back.

Bryna walked in through the kitchen door in an attempt to avoid all human contact and nearly ran smack dab into her stepbrother, Pace. Another person she *definitely* did not want to come back for.

"Where the hell were you last night?" Pace asked.

She ground her teeth and turned away from him. The only person she wanted to see less than Pace was his stupid fucking mother. At least the twins would leave her alone.

When she didn't answer, he asked, "Huh, Bri?"

She closed her eyes to try to get her emotions under control. She needed her hard exterior right now to deal with this bullshit.

"Only my friends call me Bri." She swung around and fixed him with a frosty glare that told him he was very far from a friend. "For you, Bryna will do."

"Yeah, whatever. You can't dodge my question, *Bri*."

"I don't have to answer anything. You might have left the Valley, Pace, but you're still trash to me," she spat in his face. "So, stay out of my business and out of my life."

She turned on her heel and stalked away. Thankfully, he didn't follow her. He had been a thorn in her side since he moved in. Not to mention, he was a disgusting pervert who had spent so much time gawking at her when she walked around the house that she started covering up in sweats every time, fearing she would run into him.

Halfway to the stairs, she heard the voice she had been dreading.

"There you are, Bryna, dear."

Bryna cringed and kept walking. *God, I hate my stepmother.*

"Mom, don't you think it would be nice if I drove Bryna to the game today?" Pace called, stepping out of the kitchen doorway.

Bryna stopped dead in her tracks. *Oh no, he did not just say that!*

"That would be great!" Celia said. "So sweet of you to suggest, Pace."

"I'm not going anywhere with you," Bryna said. Her eyes were icy as she scowled at the pair.

"Now, Bryna, Pace is being generous," she said as her son walked over to her.

He stared at Bryna as if he were the picture of innocence instead of the disgusting pig that he was.

"Pace wouldn't know what generous was if it bit him in the ass."

"Don't use that tone of voice with me," she said crossly.

Bryna slowly counted to three in her head. She hoped it would calm her down, but it didn't work. The anger that flooded her every time she thought about this woman in her mother's place erupted out of her.

"You are *not* my mother!"

Celia covered her mouth at the outburst, but Bryna took the opportunity to climb the remaining stairs and slam the door to her room. She had just had the most incredible night of her life, and now, she had to come back to this bullshit. As soon as she graduated, she was getting the hell out of here.

She grabbed her cheerleading uniform out of her closet and slid into the tiny gold skirt and red-and-gold cheer top. She pulled her blonde hair into a high ponytail, threw her pom-poms into her cheer bag, and then slung it over her shoulder. She was leaving now. She couldn't stand to be in this house with that woman for one more minute.

As she was tying her white shoes, Pace barged into her room.

"Ever heard of knocking, asshole?"

"Nope." He tossed himself face down onto her bed and lay there, watching her.

"You're a fucking creep. Stop staring at me like that." She stood quickly and tugged on her skirt.

"Like what?" he asked. He rolled over onto his back and stared up at her with the same greedy expression on his face.

He made her skin crawl.

She shook her head in disgust. "Why don't you get the fuck out of my room? I could have been changing."

"We're all family here."

"Just because your whore mother married my father doesn't make us family. It does make your ogling more disgusting though."

Pace just kept his eyes locked on hers. He didn't even have the decency to deny it.

"I'm getting out of here."

"You just got back."

"And?" she snapped.

"Come on, Bri. We're going to the same place, and we have to be there at the same time. Just let me drive you," Pace said.

He stood up, his six-foot-four frame towering over her. Football had padded his arms and shoulders, and standing near him made her feel tiny. She shot him a look that she hoped would make him feel just as small. Then, she left the room.

He followed her downstairs and cornered her again in the massive garage that housed all her father's prized luxury cars.

"God, what do you want?" she screamed.

"To take you to the game, Bri. Haven't you been paying attention?" He sounded so calm and controlled.

All she wanted to do was punch him in the face, but she needed to get it together. She couldn't let Pace see her flustered.

"Pace, I don't know how to make this any clearer." She balled her hands into fists. "I never want to be in the same place as you if I can ever help it."

He started laughing loudly and smiled at her revolted reaction. "It's so fun to press your buttons, *sis*." He winked before walking back inside.

She was seething.

If looks could kill, he'd already be dead.

SEVEN

THROWING HER CHEER BAG into the backseat of her Aston Martin, she slammed the door with a ferocity that would have made her dad furious. She pulled out of the garage and sped over to Harmony.

Avery and Tara were already supposed to be getting ready at school. Bryna usually strolled in right on time, looking as glamorous as ever, but she had been rushed out of the house and hadn't had the time to finish off her glamorous look, so she would have to do it in the car. She hadn't realized that stepping away from her hard shell would make it so hard to draw it back up again. She couldn't afford to be off her game today.

Before entering the building, she quickly applied a fresh coat of makeup, readjusted her ponytail, and added the signature red bow. When she went inside, she wanted them to see her as they always had.

Perfect. Queen.

Only Jude had noticed what was really stirring inside of her, and she preferred to keep it that way.

Bryna ignored the surprised stares from the rest of the team as she walked into the building early and straight to the back of the room. She tossed her bag down next to her chair and took a seat.

Avery and Tara skittered over, their brunette ponytails swishing as they moved.

"Bri!" Avery cried. "You're early."

"So observant, A," Bryna responded sarcastically.

"But, Bri, you're never early," Tara peeped.

"Why are you hovering?"

Avery and Tara immediately took a step back and started apologizing. Bryna swallowed down her frustration. She placed an amused smile on her face as they tripped over themselves to make it right.

"It's fine." Bryna held up her hand.

"So, where were you last night?" Avery asked. Her big brown doe eyes expectantly stared at her. "We waited for you at Luxe for, like, ever."

"Avery made out with Brian Blackwell," Tara rushed out.

Bryna questioningly raised her eyebrows. "You what?"

Avery flushed. "Tara is exaggerating. It was just one kiss. No big deal. It would never be serious with Brian. He's an underclassman."

"You had your tongue down his throat," Tara said.

Bryna turned her attention to Tara. "She knows her place. You can chill with the third degree."

Tara backed up another step and looked embarrassed from being called out.

Bryna's head was starting to pound. *Why do I have to deal with this petty bullshit right now?* She should have stayed in Jude's apartment and skipped the game. That sounded like heaven right about now.

"So, where were you then?" Avery repeated.

Bryna smiled up at them. She felt a victory in her hands even before she spoke the words. This was going to tighten the reins that had been slipping through her fingers ever since her father remarried.

"If you must know, I broke up with Gates last night."

Avery and Tara wore equally horrified faces.

"You did what?" Tara asked.

She stood and sighed. "I can do better."

"Better than Gates Hartman?" Avery asked.

Do I detect disbelief in my friend's voice?

"Don't you think so?" Bryna fixed them with a glare that made any response other than *yes* seem unacceptable.

"Um…yeah. Yes," Avery said.

"Of course," Tara peeped.

Bryna nodded in agreement. "I'm over the whole movie-star thing. I'd rather shop around for better merchandise."

Avery and Tara slowly bobbed their heads.

"Wow," Tara said. "You're so right. You can do better than that."

"I know."

They smiled and exchanged glances before heading back to their seats. She knew that, in a matter of minutes, the news would spread to everyone at Harmony. She tried to ignore her already beeping phone and pretended to freshen up until it was time to leave. Just as she'd expected, the whispers behind her back escalated the closer it came to departure.

Avery and Tara followed behind her as she strolled over to the state-of-the-art travel buses that would take them upstate. Before she reached the cheer bus, Pace stepped in front of them.

She could hear Avery and Tara oohing and aahing. She was going to have to knock some sense into them if they kept this up.

First, Brian, and now, Pace? Horrible, horrible taste.

"Bri, can I speak with you for a minute?" Pace asked.

She reeled in her original reaction to slap him across the face and call him out in front of everyone in the school. It wouldn't help her present situation.

"Sure, Pace. Give us a minute, girls."

They scurried onto the bus, leaving her alone with her stepbrother.

"What do you want?" she asked, dropping the act.

"You broke up with Gates?"

"What does it matter to you?"

"Sounds like some stupid rumor. Is it true?"

Breathe in. Breathe out. "Good news travels fast. Yes, I broke up with Gates last night. Now, if you'll excuse me."

She went to pass him, but he grabbed her arm.

"Is that why you were out last night?"

"Pace, if I wanted you to keep tabs on my whereabouts, I'd let you know. Until then, you can go fuck yourself." She wrenched her arm away from him. "Get out of my way."

As she was trying to leave, some of the guys from the football team barreled past them.

She pointed at his teammates. "You have a bus to catch, Pace."

"That's right. Did you hear about the talent scouts coming to the game tonight?" He paused only briefly and then continued as if he knew she wasn't going to respond, "Las Vegas State Assistant Coach Matt Cason is supposed to come watch me play."

Bryna froze.

He couldn't go to LV State.

Her mother and father had met there. He had played on the national championship football team. Her mother had been a cheerleader. Bryna had to send in her application by January for the freshman class next year. She wouldn't hear for several months, but she figured she was a shoo-in.

Pace couldn't even be considering talking to the coach about the school. She wanted to escape home...not bring it to Vegas with her.

"LV State is mine," she growled. "Don't even fucking think about it, Pace."

He smiled a toothy grin, and she stormed away, but not before she saw the challenge in his eyes.

The football game came and went with a victory led by her slimy stepbrother.

The weekend passed quickly after that, and Bryna started to grow restless. The last time she had heard from Jude was before he had walked out of his apartment. She knew the typical rule was to wait a couple of days before calling, but after the night they had shared together, how could he wait?

Three weeks of radio silence later left her stunned and pissed. She cursed herself for allowing the whole thing to mean something to her.

So what if he understood me? So what if we had an incredible night?

She had to resign herself to the fact that it had been a one-night stand.

He wasn't going to call.

EIGHT

"I THOUGHT YOU AND GATES BROKE UP," Avery whined.

Bryna rolled her baby-blues to the ceiling. *Why the hell do I have to keep having this conversation?* She and Gates were over. Just because she hadn't blabbed about it to *People* magazine didn't make it any less true.

"We are," Bryna snapped.

"Then, why is he signing autographs outside of school?"

Bryna jerked her head to the front of the parking lot, and her eyes bulged.

Fucking hell! What the fuck is he doing here?
This will not do.
This will not do at all.

She reeled in her state of shock. Breaking up with Gates had given her the leverage she needed. She was too good for Gates Hartman.

But maybe she could spin this. If it looked like he was chasing her…well, all the better.

"Gates Hartman," she said idly. She languidly strolled down the stairs and out of Harmony Prep as if seeing her ex-boyfriend outside of the building was an every day occurrence.

Avery trailed behind her, and she would bet anything that Tara was close by. As Bryna walked forward, the sea of girls in front of Gates parted like she truly was royalty. Too bad Gates wasn't her Prince Charming. But he would do for now.

He smiled that gorgeous grin solely for her, and all the girls sighed as they dreamily stared up at him.

Good luck if they ever thought they would get someone like Gates.

Dear Lord, he was handsome. No wonder he had won America's heart on the big screen. That face was downright delicious. She didn't want to be distracted from her mission, so she purposefully avoided looking at anything but his liquid blue eyes.

"Hey, Bri," Gates said completely nonchalant. "You ready to go?"

She placed a curious smile on her face and planted her hand on one hip. "Where exactly are we going?"

He crossed his arms over his chest and leaned back against the hood of his fire red Porsche convertible. The look on his face screamed loud and clear: don't-start-this-shit-with-me.

She just arched an eyebrow in a silent rebuttal. *You started this, and I'm going to finish it.*

"I've been gone on set for too long. Came straight here to see my girl." He straightened and reached a hand out to her. He was so matter-of-fact as if she hadn't broken up with him while he had been gone and she hadn't fucked some other guy.

She looked down at his hand and debated. *Honestly, what does he expect me to do?* There was no way she was giving into this so easily. She kept her face firmly blank as she returned her eyes to his. "But I haven't been your girl in three weeks."

The crowd shifted awkwardly and looked around at others in disbelief. They were surprised that anyone whether Queen bee or not would turn down Gates Hartman. People gasped and started whispering behind their hands to each other.

Let this be a lesson.

Gates appeared oblivious to everyone's reactions. Though she knew that he was enjoying the attention. He had always been comfortable in front of crowds. "Yeah. Okay, Bri," he said, disbelievingly. He even rolled his eyes for good measure. "We're together. You know it's true. I know it's true. Everyone else here knows we're together. That's not stopping because of a phone call. You're my girl. Now let's get out of here."

Everyone glanced at her expectantly. She wondered if they thought this had all been a stunt. It wasn't, but they probably thought so. She had legitimately broken up with Gates for Jude, the asshole who had never called her back. But she wasn't about to tell them about Jude. In fact, she hadn't told anyone about Jude. She couldn't trust anyone with that information. Only Gates knew that she had gone home with someone that night and that was the way it was going to stay. Not that it really mattered anymore since Jude still hadn't bothered to call.

With a resigned sigh, she finally placed her hand in his. It wouldn't matter if she spent time with Gates if there was no one else in her life. Plus, it would look good to leave with him. "Fine. We'll talk about this later," she admonished.

Gates pulled her close, planted a kiss on her temple, and then helped her into the passenger seat of his convertible. He nodded at the girls still gawking at him, walked around the car, and then hopped over the door into the driver's seat.

Show-off.

They pulled out of the parking lot, and she immediately turned to him in frustration. "That was a dirty trick you pulled."

He smirked. "How else was I going to get you to come to my place?"

"*Your* place?" she asked. "I am *not* going to your place."

"Oh? We're already on our way. And it's for the better, right? Otherwise, I would have had to throw you over my shoulder and tie you to my bed to get you to talk to me," he said, his blue eyes shining with glee. "Now, I know you would have just *hated* that. Wouldn't you have, Bri?"

She glared at him harder. The goddamn man knew her too well. "Don't fucking kid yourself, Gates."

"Well, you're coming to my place whether you want to or not. So, you can wipe off that eat-shit look on your face."

"Whatever. We're not even together anymore."

"A phone call three weeks ago at four o'clock in the morning isn't enough to end things with me, Bri. I'm not one of your pets or one of your goddamn followers."

She huffed and looked away from him. Her hair whipped all around her head as Gates navigated the traffic into Los Angeles in silence and then pulled into the gated community where he lived.

Once his car was parked, he guided her straight up to his bedroom and shut the door behind her. She beelined for the bathroom to check out what the convertible had done to her hair. As she'd suspected, she looked like a hot mess. She finger-combed the tangled tresses.

"Bri," Gates groaned, leaning against the doorframe.

"What?" she asked. She definitely needed a brush to fix the rest of the damage.

"I've been gone a long time." He walked up behind her and slid his hand across her stomach. She shouldered him aside as she worked on her hair some more.

"And?"

"Too damn long," he murmured. He ignored her attempts to dislodge him and kissed along her shoulder.

"What do you want, Gates?" she snapped.

He grabbed her by the arm and swung her to face him. "I don't think you're listening, babe."

"No, I don't think *you're* listening! If you think that cornering me at school and dragging me to your house is going to change what I said, then you're wrong. I told you, we are through. I don't care if it was on the phone, where you were, what time it was. It's over."

His hands slid down her arms and wrapped around her waist. "I shouldn't have to fight this hard for you to want this."

"Just because *you* can't get other pussy doesn't mean I can't get other cock," she said, arching an eyebrow. It was a low dig, even for her. Hardly even true, but she couldn't help herself.

But he smirked insufferably. "Bri, cut the shit. You and I both know, pussy is easy to come by."

His hand went to the front of her skintight black jeans. He snapped the button, dragged the zipper down, and had his hand inside her panties before she could move away. A moan escaped her lips as he swirled his finger around her.

"But you're different," he whispered into her ear. "I want you."

"Fuck, Gates." She stumbled back a step and shook her head. "You're not listening."

"No, I'm not fucking listening." He easily cleared the distance and scooped her up into his arms.

Christ, when did he get so strong? He'd been able to lift her before, but now, he carried her as if she weighed no more than a feather.

He tossed her back on the bed, and as he stripped his shirt off, she really took notice.

He looked like he had been in the gym every waking moment when he wasn't filming. She knew that the film needed him to be bigger, but fuck, he had sculpted abs, built arms, and that wonderful V leading—

No, she was not going to look lower.

Okay. So, she looked lower. And damn.

Fuck, he had always been good-looking, but now…he was off the charts.

His eyes turned into molten lava when he caught her watching him. He was one cocky motherfucker. His pants followed his shirt, and then he was yanking her jeans off her body.

She should have stopped him and made him reconsider. She had fucked Jude three weeks ago. She had wanted it. She still wanted it. But she had put the ball in his court, and he hadn't called her. No one did that to Bryna Turner. Of course, he didn't know who she really was. That didn't matter though, because they'd had an amazing time, and she had put on a spectacular performance. Now, she was left wondering why the hell he wasn't interested.

"Wait," she cried, realizing Gates's lips were crawling up her leg. "I slept with someone else."

Gates sat back and fixed his gaze on her. "I gathered that, based on our conversation."

She glared at him. "Why don't you care about that?"

"Because I fucked some other girl after." He shrugged. "Didn't fucking mean anything, Bri. Just made me miss you. So, now, I'm home, and I want you. I want *my* girl."

Bryna slapped him across the face. "You said we never broke up!"

He grabbed her hand and pushed it down. "And you fucking said we did."

"You can't have it both ways, Gates! You can't fuck some bitch and claim that she didn't mean anything, and then come crawling back to me. That's not how this fucking works, you prick!" She wriggled

45

out of his grasp and sat up on the bed. What an arrogant ass!

"What?" he growled, grabbing her wrists again. She tried to move away from him but he held her steady. "You think you can decide when we're over and fuck someone, but as soon as I do, you decide to slap me? Fuck that, Bri. I've known you for too damn long not to know your games when I see one. I'm not a game. You break up with me to fuck some other dude, then you have to fucking know I'm going to do whatever the fuck I want."

She shook her head furiously. "Let me go, Gates. Let me go, and get the fuck off of me!"

"You are never going to find anyone who gets your insanity as much as I do." He wasn't just angry. He was pissed. She could see him gaining momentum in his argument. "And I don't just like it. It fucking turns me on. So, get it out of your head that this changes shit."

"I know exactly how much this changes things." Her breathing was heavy, her chest heaving, as she pursed her lips and narrowed her eyes.

He looked murderous. His eyes were blazing, and his hands were tightening around her small wrists.

Then, as if the dam broke, his lips were on hers. Their bodies tangled together, and a heated fury seemed to sweep over them, pounding through their veins and overtaking their senses.

Gates ripped her shirt over her head and then removed the remainder of their clothing. Suddenly, the air was thick in the room, and she had trouble breathing. The sexual tension was high. Thoughts shattered as desire took over.

He surged into her, and there was only feeling.

The feel of his body pressed against her, driving into her. The feel of their skin damp with sweat. The feel of him sliding in and out, bringing her to new heights, with the practiced ease of someone who knew her body.

Then, the feel of release, and everything else came back.

The sound of her screams and his grunts of ecstasy. The look of victory that shot across his face. The taste and smell of sex in the air.

Gates rolled over next to her and sighed. "That's my girl."

NINE

"I'M GLAD YOU FINALLY CAME TO YOUR SENSES," Gates said.

He sauntered into her bedroom in a tuxedo. His dark hair was perfectly tousled, and he was sporting some well-groomed scruff that he claimed was necessary since he had to be clean-shaven on set.

"Just because I'm going to this party with you does *not* mean I've come to my senses," Bryna said, rolling her eyes. She was going because Jude still hadn't fucking called, and being around Gates was so easy.

"Whatever you have to tell yourself."

She ignored him and twirled in place. "Well, how do I look?" She had picked out a floor-length white lace gown with a plunge neckline and a slit that ran up to her upper thigh on one side.

"Perfect," he murmured. "It's just…"

"What?"

He sent her a bemused smile. "Virginal white?"

"Well, I am so pure." Bryna slid her hand up her exposed thigh.

His eyes followed the movement, and he stepped toward her.

"I could remind you just how pure you are," he said, backing her up into the trifold mirror.

Bryna held her head high and gave him a detached look. "Maybe later."

"I'm taking you up on that. I've been back for two weeks. This cat-and-mouse game has gone on long enough."

She batted her eyes lashes. "I've no idea what you mean."

She brushed past him and then dropped her seductive smile. She had been conflicted about things with Gates since he got back. They had slept together that first day, and even though they had been together a handful of times since then, she was still holding him back and making him work for it.

She just couldn't stop thinking about Jude. She knew it was ridiculous. He'd never called, which meant he wasn't interested. Still, she felt like there had been a connection, one she was lacking with Gates. And she didn't want to lead Gates on. She would always care about him, but she was starting to see more and more that the breakup hadn't been just because she wanted to sleep with someone else.

"I'm sure you don't," Gates said, grabbing her ass, before they walked through the door.

Gates had rented a limo for the occasion, and they sipped champagne on the way into the city. Bryna was pleasantly buzzed by the time they reached the venue. Once they pulled up to the entrance, she stepped out of the limo and into a world of glitz and glamour.

The club was a known celebrity hotspot, so paparazzi always staked out the entrance. A velvet rope held back a line full to bursting. Gates slid out of the car behind her, casually draping his arm around her waist. At a glance, the ushers opened the doors, and they were whisked inside.

The lights were low, the music served as a seductive backbeat, and the people were more beautiful than ever.

Gates guided her over to the bar where he ordered her a dirty martini and got himself a beer. She let her eyes wander the crowd. She knew the cast of Gates's latest film, *Broken Road*, was planning to meet up here now that they were all back in Los Angeles. She had heard that, when they had completed the filming in Savannah, the production team had thrown an insane wrap party. She was surprised that Gates had returned so soon afterward. By the way he'd told the story, he should have had a three-day hangover.

Her eyes landed on a brunette in the midst of an adoring crowd. Bryna smiled and pulled Gates over to toward his costar, Chloe Avana.

"Chloe!" Bryna cried, wrapping her arms around the small girl.

She was even shorter than Bryna with long luscious hair and big brown eyes. She had started acting at a young age, and after a successful stint on Disney, she had landed the lead across from Gates. Not only was she already a good actress, she could also belt out songs like Christina Aguilera.

Bryna didn't get along with many girls, so she had been shocked to find that she actually liked Chloe.

They had hung out a bunch when she came into town to visit Gates and lounge around set.

"Bri! It's so good to see you," Chloe said. "When did you get here?"

"We just showed up."

"Good. I'm glad he got you to come out tonight."

Bryna shrugged. "Of course I came out. Why wouldn't I?"

No need for Chloe to know anything was different between her and Gates. She could put on a front for anyone.

"Just glad you're here. Let's go somewhere, so we can catch up." Chloe looped their arms together, and they walked into a private sitting room. "Tell me everything. How is life? How is Harmony? Sometimes, I wish I had stayed in school. I hate tutors."

"Life is great, and Harmony is even better," Bryna lied. She doubted Chloe really wanted to hear about high school drama. She might wish she was in high school, but it wasn't as if she didn't already have her dream job. "What about you? How was filming?"

Chloe sighed happily. "Grueling but the most amazing experience. I can't wait to see the final cut. You should come with me to look at dresses for the premiere," Chloe said eagerly. "By the way, your gown is so fabulous."

"Thank you. Are you going to model an original?"

Chloe nodded. "I'm supposed to be getting samples in soon, so the designer can finalize the product based on my measurements, and then Gates and I will go on the first wave of the promotion tour."

Bryna's gaze drifted to Gates questioningly. She hadn't heard anything about a promotional tour. Of course, she knew that actors typically went on one, but still he hadn't said anything.

Gates shrugged. "We just got the itinerary today."

Right.

Bryna's phone buzzing in her clutch kept her from offering up some fake response. She doubted he had just gotten it in today, but she didn't have the time at the moment to figure out why if he was being all lovey-dovey that he hadn't told her when he was leaving town again.

She pulled it out of her bag. She didn't recognize the number, but she didn't want to think about Gates leaving again. Even if they were in a weird place, it was still Gates.

She held it up for Chloe to see. "I have to take this. I'll catch up with you later."

"Bri," Gates said, grabbing her arm.

"I'll talk to you when I get off the phone."

"I just got the itinerary," he repeated.

She arched an eyebrow. "You said as much. Can I take my call now?"

"Fine." He took a step back, but still looked disgruntled.

Bryna stepped out of the room and found a corner near the restrooms where it was relatively quiet. "Hello?"

"Hey, gorgeous. Did you miss me?"

Bryna's heart stopped. "Jude?"

TEN

"GOOD TO HEAR YOUR VOICE, BRI. I've been thinking about you," Jude responded.

She ground her teeth together and tried to think of a reason not to lay into him for making her wait five fucking weeks without so much as a text message.

But she couldn't find one.

"Oh, you've been thinking about me? That's sweet," she purred. "After five weeks without a call, I kind of forgot about you."

"I'm sure," he said disbelievingly. "What are you doing tonight?"

"I'm not some booty call," she said defensively. "I'm hanging up now." Hanging up was the last thing she wanted to do, but she wanted him to beg for it. "Good night, Jude."

"Bri, wait."

She shook her head. She should have just ended it. She didn't need a guy who couldn't be bothered to call her, who obviously didn't feel the same way she did. "Give me one reason I shouldn't hang up on you."

"If you wanted to, then you would have already hung up on me."

Point. But she didn't want to concede it.

"A real reason," she said. Her voice was like ice.

"I want to see you again."

She scoffed, "That's cute."

"And you want to see me again, too."

"Do not presume to know what I do or do not want," Bryna spat. "It's been five weeks. I'm not interested."

"I have a job that takes me out of town for extended periods of time."

Bryna gasped mockingly. "A job that demands no cell phone use? Shocking."

She could almost feel his frustration through the phone.

"I had access to a phone. I just didn't call you."

"Obviously," she snapped. At least he had finally admitted that he had just avoided calling her for all that time. "Now, excuse me, I can make better use of my time elsewhere."

"Bri," he pleaded, "I'm only in town tonight. Come see me."

She shook her head in frustration. *The nerve of this guy.* She didn't care what kind of connection she had thought they had. No one treated Bryna Turner like this.

"Please. Don't insult me. I'm not interested in another one-night stand."

"No one said anything about a one-night stand."

"Forgive me if I don't believe you."

Five weeks had been long enough to realize he wasn't going to call. Now that he had, he was only interested in a booty call. She didn't know why this upset her so much. When she'd left the club with him, she had known that they were going to have sex, but she had fooled herself into believing there was more between them when there was nothing. She had thought that when she left her number, he would call, like every other guy she had ever been interested in had done. She didn't like making herself vulnerable to people who would later throw it back in her face with their silence.

And now this call...

"No, Jude, I can't think of a single reason to come see you tonight. Find someone else."

She ended the call before he could respond. She was finally getting back to her life and trying to forget the man who had made her feel different...the man who had seen the truth about her. She had lied on the phone when she said she hadn't been thinking about him. It was even making her doubt Gates.

Fucking idiot.

Walking back to the room where she had left Gates, she found it empty. She scrunched her brows together. *Where did he go?*

She asked the closest person if he had seen him and followed his directions up the stairs. Voices traveled down to her as she neared the landing.

"But I *hate* lying," Chloe said.

"You're not lying. You're not saying anything. It's just like we discussed." Gates's voice carried.

Bryna crossed her arms. *Lying about what?*

"Am I just supposed to be friends with her? When she's being all friendly to me, I look at her and just burst at the seams, wanting to tell her," Chloe admitted.

"Chloe, you know we can't tell anyone what happened."

Bryna couldn't stand there and listen to this any longer. She'd heard enough. "Well, if you didn't want anyone to hear, then you probably shouldn't be having this conversation in a nightclub," she said, walking up the last remaining stairs.

Chloe covered her mouth. She looked frightened and pitifully young. "Bri, I am so sorry."

Gates frowned. "I don't know what you think you heard, but—"

"But what, Gates?" she asked. She didn't want to hear any of his excuses or lies. She just wanted to have everything out in the open. "I'm assuming that the girl you slept with is Chloe—the one you swore to me meant nothing and just reminded you of how much you missed me."

"You said that?" Chloe whispered. She sounded horrified.

"I couldn't tell you who it was," Gates said. He looked like a mouse caught in a trap.

"Right. Because I'd rush to the media?" Bryna asked, rolling her eyes. "So, who should I call first? TMZ or *People* magazine?"

Gates cringed. "You wouldn't."

"Hell hath no fury like a woman scorned."

Chloe reached out and grasped Bryna's hand. "Bri, you have to know how sorry I am. I never would have come between you. Gates said that you broke up."

Bryna shook her hand off. She stared down at Chloe with the detached cold anger that always bubbled just under the surface, and Chloe shrank away. The girl didn't know what Bryna was capable of. She wasn't queen bee for nothing. She hadn't survived in Hollywood for nothing either.

She turned her focus back on Gates, and he levelly met her gaze.

"We were broken up even though he tried to convince me that we weren't. He's been trying to convince me ever since he got home. Who knew it was just a guilty conscience?" She tapped her lips twice in disgust.

He tilted his head down and looked at her in exasperation. "You slept with someone else, too," Gates reminded her.

"Don't get me started," Bryna snapped at him. "I called you in the middle of the night and told you the truth. I was going home with him. It was over. You were the one who came home, told me the girl meant nothing, and were doing everything to make us work. What were you so afraid of that you couldn't tell me it was Chloe?"

He glanced toward Chloe and then back to Bryna. "Please don't do this."

"I'll let you figure it out for yourself, Gates. We're through."

Bryna rushed back down the stairs in a hurry. She had said everything she wanted to say to them. There was a difference between what she had done and what Gates had done. Why was it so difficult to be honest with her? Gates clearly had feelings for Chloe or he wouldn't have hid the fact.

Once she reached the exit to the club, she realized to her surprise that Gates hadn't followed after her. She ground her teeth together in anger.

She fished out her phone and dialed Jude's number. "Where am I meeting you?"

ELEVEN

BRYNA HAD BEEN THINKING ABOUT THIS MOMENT for weeks.

Jude opened the door to his apartment with a smile that took her breath away. *Shit. He is gorgeous.*

"Bri." His eyes traveled over her stunning evening gown, and he raised his eyebrows. "I feel a tad underdressed."

She surveyed him with approval trying to not showcase her eagerness. He was in nice slacks, a button-up, and a silk tie.

"Just a tad."

"Come in." He stepped back and let her walk past him into the apartment.

She held her head high, holding on to her illusion of control. She needed to keep her wits about her and not fall for his game. This time it was going to be different. Their relationship and everything that consisted of would be on her terms, and she wasn't going to be the one left waiting again.

"Where did you come from, wearing a dress like *that*?"

She raised an eyebrow at him. "Are we answering questions now? I thought you liked the mystery."

"Let me guess," he said, walking toward her until only inches separated them. "A Black-tie formal event. Your boyfriend took you as arm candy."

"Close," she purred.

"On what part?"

"Ex-boyfriend." She pursed her lips and shook her head. "Is this really what you want to be talking about?"

"Just attempting to figure out why you called me back."

Jude ran his hand down her arm and stared at her questioningly. All she wanted to do was keep her guard up, but with one look, he was shattering her resolve. *How does he do that?*

"And I'm trying to figure out why you called at all," she managed to get out. Despite her best efforts, her voice was breathy.

"I called because I've been thinking about you. Simple as that."

She scoffed and stepped away from him. *Spell broken. Does he think I'm an idiot? If he's been thinking about me, then why didn't he call five weeks ago?*

She stalked across the room to his wet bar and began to pour herself a glass of scotch.

"By all means, treat yourself."

"Thank you. I will," she said with a cheeky smile. She deliberately took a long gulp before turning back to face him. "Now, you were saying something?"

"Bri, get your ass over here." He pointed at the spot in front of him.

"Excuse me?"

"You heard me. Get your ass over here *now*."

"Who do you think you are, talking to me like that?" she asked, not moving an inch.

"This is my booty call, right?" Jude raised his eyebrows at her.

Bryna set the glass down and crossed her arms. "I think you have things all wrong."

"Do I?"

"I'm no one's booty call. When I called you back, you became mine," she told him with a devilish smile.

He chuckled softly at her response. "Well, in that case…"

Suddenly, she was slammed backward into the scotch cabinet. His arm swept the crystal glasses to the side. One fell to the ground and smashed at her feet. All she could do was giggle. His lips landed on top of hers, hungry and desperate. She could feel the need of the past five weeks between them in that one kiss. She might have been able to fool him into believing that she hadn't cared about their time apart but not after that kiss.

His fingers dug into her bare thigh, exposed from the slit in her dress. Then, he was pushing the expensive material aside, sliding his hands under her thighs and hoisting her on top of the counter. Jude pulled back to yank her underwear down, and then he unbuttoned his pants and dropped them to the ground.

Their lips crashed together again as he thrust his fingers up into her.

He groaned into her mouth. "You're so wet."

"I might have had some fun in the limo before I got here."

He wrenched back and looked into her playful blue eyes. "You masturbated before you got here?"

"As if you haven't at the thought of me," she purred.

It made her laugh to think that she had masturbated in Gates's limo before coming over to see Jude.

"Oh, I have," he said, slipping his fingers in and out of her. "It's just so hot to think about you doing it."

"Well, if you're a good boy, maybe I'll let you watch." She winked and then tipped her head back as his fingers worked their magic.

He slipped out of her, and a second later, his cock slammed filled her. She gasped at the abrupt change. *Fuck, he has a huge dick.*

He shoved into her again, harder than the last time, and then he leaned in close. "I guess I'm not going to get to watch because I only intend to be very, *very* bad." He punctuated his last words with rough thrusts.

She moaned in pleasure. This was just what she needed after the night she'd had. No, this was what she needed all the time. She needed to forget about Gates and high school and her parents and Pace and everything else in her life and get lost in this fantasy. Get lost in Jude.

He grabbed a fistful of her hair and yanked her head back to expose her neck. He nipped at the bare skin until it was red and raw. All the while, he was keeping up a steady rhythm, bringing her closer to climax. She could feel the weeks of pent-up frustration washing off of them. Sure, she had been with Gates, but that hardly compared to this. Nothing had ever compared to this.

"Harder," she moaned. She wanted it to be so deep, so rough, so hard that she wouldn't have to feel anything anymore, except for this.

Jude let go of her hair and smirked down at her. The look he gave her said that he accepted the challenge. A second later, he hoisted her off the counter and threw her down onto the plush carpet. He was back inside her immediately, lifting both of her legs onto his shoulders, tipping her hips off the ground, and then pounding into her as hard as he could.

She cried out as she crossed the line between pleasure and pain. But she didn't stop him. She liked this. She wanted this.

Fuck, she was about to come.

The orgasm rocked her body like an explosion bursting in the night sky. Her eyes fluttered, and her toes curled. She was seeing stars as her chest heaved, and she lay on the floor, panting.

Jude came after her release, falling on top of her.

"Oh my God," she murmured.

"What you said," he said.

"I'm glad I'm flexible." She slowly removed her legs from his shoulders and dropped them on either side of his body. They felt like Jell-O and shook of their own accord. She was a little worried about having to walk anywhere.

He swept her blonde hair out of her face, kissed her swollen lips, and then just smiled down at her with so much affection on his face.

"What?" she murmured.

"You're so beautiful."

She sighed contentedly. "Not the reaction I thought I'd get from a comment about flexibility, but I approve."

He laughed and kissed her on the nose. "We have all night to investigate this flexibility."

"Uh, I don't think so."

Bryna rolled out from under him, stood on her wobbly legs, and adjusted her dress. She was sure her hair looked completely unruly from the carpet, her makeup was all messed up, and her underwear were tattered and discarded. She couldn't even see where Jude had thrown them. Not to mention, the state of her neck. She was doubtful that she was going to be able to conceal his handiwork. That's probably what he wanted in the first place.

Jude rose to his feet as well and tugged on his boxer briefs. "You want to leave?" he asked in disbelief.

"You ran out on me last time," she reminded him. *Aha!* There were her underwear. She grabbed them off the ground and slid them back on. "It's only fitting that I get the five-week break this time."

He looked down at this feet and then back up at her. He seemed hesitant, almost uncertain, and apologetic. "I really was out of town this whole time."

"That's not an explanation. That's an excuse. So, I'm going to go now."

It was the last thing she wanted to do after having the most amazing sex with him, but she couldn't let him think that she was nothing better than a one-night stand or a booty call. That wasn't what she wanted. She enjoyed the sex, and while it might be some of the best sex she'd ever had, she could still get sex elsewhere. That was what she had told Gates too.

She had enjoyed her time with Jude because she thought there was a connection. Without that connection, it was...just meaningless sex.

Amazing meaningless sex.

She turned on her heel, retrieved her discarded clutch, and walked to the door.

Jude grabbed her arm before she could reach it. "Bri, this isn't why I called you over."

"You didn't want to have sex with me? I beg to differ."

"I did. Of course I did. How could I not? But I called because I wanted to see you. I've been thinking about you a lot. In fact, I can't get you out of my head," he told her. He ran a hand down her arm and drew her closer. "Ever since that night, I thought it would be easier to forget you. I'm separated from my wife, but I'm married to my work. I won't bore you with the details. Despite all that, I still called you tonight and not for sex, but for this."

He walked over to his suit jacket hanging on a stand next to the door and retrieved a red box from the pocket. Bryna froze. She would recognize that box *anywhere*. Even before the gold lettering came into focus, she knew what it said on the top.

Cartier.

Words failed her as he opened the box to reveal the most gorgeous chandelier diamond earrings she had ever seen. She had a small collection of jewelry that she had acquired over the years, but most of the good stuff had belonged to her mother. Anything else she coveted her father usually rented for her for special occasions. She owned absolutely nothing like this.

"I couldn't stop thinking about you. I knew that I needed to make this right, and I wanted to start by getting you something almost as beautiful as you are."

She reached out and brushed the gorgeous earrings. "You got these for me?"

"Yes."

She took them out of the box, placed the new earrings in her ears, and examined them in the mirror. "They look stunning," she whispered.

"As do you."

"Thank you." She truly was at a loss for words. What else could she say as she stared at her reflection in the mirror?

Her heart pounded in her chest. It wasn't often that she was wrong about people. If Jude had planned this all along, then she hadn't just been wrong. She had been out of the park, blinded.

"I want to keep seeing you, Bri. My job keeps me busy, but when I'm in town, I want to spend my time with you."

TWELVE

BRYNA WAS ALMOST FINISHED with her game-day makeup when her phone buzzed next to her.

> *Change of plans. I'm in town tonight not tomorrow. Meet at my place?*

"Shit!" she cried.

Jude's text could not have come at a worse time.

For the past couple of weeks, they had been seeing each other whenever he was in town. Primarily, they would spend their time locked away in his bedroom, but he was supposed to take her out tomorrow night. She had no intention of missing that opportunity.

The only problem was, she had a football game tonight. There were only two home games left in the season, and then she would be done. They would have the state championship and then some competitions in the spring, but tonight was one of her last chances to cheer at Harmony. Not to mention, she had never missed a game before. If she didn't show up, everyone would freak out.

But she couldn't get enough time with Jude.

A night here. Half a day there.

She wanted more.

> *I have a commitment. I'll get back to you.*

She sent the message and then completed her makeup. She couldn't believe she was even contemplating missing the game, yet all she wanted to do was head over to Jude's place right now.

> *I'll make it worth your time.*

She smirked at the message. *You'd better.*

> *Get out of it for me?*

> *You don't even know what it is.*

> *Does it matter? You would tell me if you wanted me to know. I just want to see you.*

She sighed. *What's one game anyway?*

> *I'll see what I can do.*

First, she needed to get herself out of her responsibilities as captain of the cheerleading squad. Everyone was going to flip, but they would just have to deal. She had never missed a game before, but there was a first time for everything. After she worked that out, she had to reason a way out of getting out of the house unnoticed by her family.

Bryna pressed the speed dial for Avery's phone and waited for her to answer.

"Bri! Hey!"

She dived right in. No pretenses. All business. "I have to miss the game tonight. So, you're in charge in my stead. Don't fuck this up, and really try to do some justice to my title."

"Wait, what?" Avery asked in disbelief.

"Are you suddenly deaf?"

"No. No. Sorry, Bri. I just…you've never missed a game." She sounded frantic and panicky.

"Which is why you are going to have to do a spectacular job tonight or else I'll have to reconsider your spot as my number two."

"Of course. I'll do what I can," Avery answered immediately. "But what's wrong? Are you all right? Did something happen?"

Bryna shook her head. Honestly, she could do without the questions. "I'm sick."

"But you were feeling fine this afternoon in class."

"Avery, stop with the third degree. I'm sick and can't make the game. That's all. I'll see you on Monday."

Bryna hung up the phone in frustration. She hadn't thought it would be that difficult to miss the game. Shaking off Avery's concern, she dialed the number for the cheerleading coach, Coach Baker. She gave a slightly more believable excuse for her absence, and by the end of the conversation, the coach was completely supportive of her staying at home and taking it easy. *Perfect.*

She was changing out of her uniform when Pace barged into her room.

"Jesus, Pace!" She quickly turned around and threw on a T-shirt.

"What are you doing?" he asked, stopping in the doorway.

"I was fucking changing."

His eyes glanced down at the discarded uniform. "Why?"

"I don't feel well. I'm staying home. I put Avery in charge."

"No, really. Why?" he asked disbelievingly.

She rolled her eyes and crossed her arms. "Because I'm sick, you idiot. Now, get out of my room before I cough on you, and you catch it. Don't want Harmony to miss their star quarterback, do you?" she asked sarcastically.

"You would have to be laid out and dying to miss a game, and you're standing here, arguing with me." He looked at her questioningly. He clearly didn't believe a thing she had said.

"Well, I must be dying because I'm not fucking going." She walked across the room and shoved him through the door. "So, leave me alone," she said, slamming the door in his face.

Bryna breathed a sigh of relief. She jotted out a text to Jude, letting him know that she would be there within the hour. After waiting for Pace to leave the house, she slipped into a slinky gold dress and black booties, and then she disappeared from the house.

Jude wanted their first public outing to be a surprise.

Bryna assumed it would be somewhere fancy, preferably an upscale expensive restaurant in West Hollywood. When he pulled up outside of Aim, her heart started hammering wildly in her chest. She definitely had *not* expected him to choose a place where she could have been found with Gates when they were together. She couldn't be seen by anyone who might recognize her, not when she was lying about being sick to miss the football game.

Luckily, Gates was out of Los Angeles, on tour promoting *Broken Road*, and all her friends who might have also been at Aim were currently at the football game she was skipping. It made her antsy to be on her home turf, but the likelihood that someone would recognize her was slim. At least she hoped so.

Jude valeted his Jaguar and helped her out of the passenger seat. Then, they walked into the restaurant. As Jude spoke with the hostess, Bryna carefully surveyed the room for anyone she knew.

The restaurant was small and intimate in the front with a back room for large parties. It was all modern décor with high ceilings, plush white padded booths, and minimalistic decorations. As far as she could tell, she didn't recognize anyone. It had been a while since she had been here anyway. Maybe her luck was with her.

"Right this way," the hostess said, directing them to a booth in the back.

Bryna took a seat facing the room, so she could see if anyone she knew came in the door. She didn't mind being seen with Jude as long as he didn't find out how old she was, and it didn't interfere with cheer. Either of those things could be potentially catastrophic.

"Bri?"

"Yes?" she asked, snapping out of her trance.

"You seem out of it," Jude said. His hand rested comfortably on her waist, bringing her back to reality. "Is everything okay?"

She nodded confidently. She couldn't let him know how out of her element she was at the moment. "Of course. I just wasn't expecting Aim."

"You've been here before?" He sounded surprised.

"I've been everywhere in Los Angeles," she said mysteriously.

He arched an eyebrow. "That's a sidestep if I've ever heard one."

She fluttered her eyelashes and gave him a sly look. "Doesn't sound like me at all."

He laughed and looked down at the menu. She followed suit and sighed quietly in relief that he hadn't pushed the subject.

When the waiter came over to take their order, Jude requested a bottle of red wine along with their meal, and then they were left alone once more.

"I'm glad we were able to do this tonight," Jude said.

"Me, too."

"I haven't dated in a long time, Bri, but I really want this to work, and I'd like to get to know you better."

A smile lit up her face. He wanted to move forward with their relationship. The earrings were the first step, then going out on their first real date, and now, this.

It had been fun, concealing her identity thus far, but she *was* curious about him. She wasn't ready to tell him about Harmony yet. She needed to be secure in their relationship before she let him know that she was in high school...or that she was only seventeen. *Small, minor details for later.*

"So, we can start out slow and figure this thing out as we go," he suggested.

"I think I'd like that."

"I thought this could be the beginning of slow," he said with a wink. He produced a flat square Tiffany's box from his jacket pocket and slid it across the table.

Bryna slowly reached forward and took the box in her hand. *This is slow?*

"If Tiffany's and Cartier are slow, what is fast going to be? A private jet and a weekend in Saint Barts?"

He chuckled and gestured for her to open it. "I like to give gifts, and since you obviously love the earrings I got you"—her hand went to the diamond earrings in her ears—"I wanted to get you something to match."

Bryna slid the white ribbon off the box and lifted the lid. Inside was a slim bangle with inlaid diamonds. It was so perfect and elegant. She slipped it onto her wrist and stared at the way it glittered and sparkled in the light. Completely classic and timeless, she could wear it with anything.

"I love it."

"Good." Jude reached across the table and took her hand in his. He gently ran his thumb across her wrist where the bangle rested, taking in all the diamonds shining from the jewelry he had bought her.

Shortly afterward, their food arrived. They ate while chatting about their shared love of sports cars and college football. Bryna didn't tell him *why* she loved Las Vegas State so much or that she hadn't gone there, but it didn't stop her from giving him shit about the fact that he had graduated from their biggest rival, University of Southern California.

After they finished their bottle of wine, Jude paid the check, and they were on their way out the door to return to his place.

A woman called out from a table near the door, "Bri!"

Bryna stopped and turned to face the woman. She silently prayed it wasn't anyone from Harmony. That would be a tough fucking thing to explain away. When she got a glimpse of the person, she realized that she didn't recognize the stranger at all. *How the hell does this person know me?*

"Hey!" Bryna said with false enthusiasm.

The woman stood and gave her a hug. "I haven't seen you in forever."

"Yeah, I've been so swamped."

"I heard about you and—" She stopped, looked up at Jude, and then bit her lip. "Well, I see you've moved on."

Bryna shrugged noncommittally. So, this woman knew her through Gates. At least she had stopped herself from saying his name. *How many Gates are there in the city?*

"Anyway, so good to see you again. Next time you're out, stop by the club." She stuffed a business card into Bryna's hand. "Bring your new boyfriend, too. I'm sure Max will put you on the list."

Max was a promoter friend of Bryna's who would get her into all the hottest nightclubs. Bryna glanced down at the woman's card. *Dee Zion.* No recognition. *Must just be a club promoter. Phew!*

"Will do, Dee. Thanks," Bryna said before leaving her behind.

Jude looked at her questioningly as they waited for the valet to bring around his car. "Who was that?"

"Honestly, I have no clue."

"She clearly knew you."

Bryna shrugged. "That happens sometimes."

He narrowed his eyes and seemed to assess her. "You know, when we first met, I thought you looked familiar."

"I get that a lot, too."

"You aren't some hot model or actress I should know about who will make me feel stupid for not recognizing earlier, are you?"

"Why? Because I wear nice shoes and always carry my passport?" she joked.

"Oh, fuck. You are, aren't you?"

He actually looked a little afraid for a second before she broke down laughing.

"No. I'm not a model or actress. I'm just me, and that's good enough for the attention."

"Good enough for me, too," he said, opening the car door when it rolled up and helping her inside.

THIRTEEN

"YES, MRS. MATHISON, I completely understand the amount of work it would take to lead the Pink Charity Benefit for Harmony. But I also know that I am exactly the girl for the job."

"I believe you, Bryna," Mrs. Mathison said, leaning back in her desk chair. "I just wanted to be sure. I know that your extracurricular schedule is already full, and the Pink Charity Benefit is Harmony's biggest philanthropy event of the year."

Bryna smiled sweetly as she uncrossed and crossed her legs. "I am always willing to take on more to further my charitable contribution. I hardly consider it work at all."

Running the largest benefit of the year would look stellar on her college applications, and she wanted to make sure everything would be in place for her. Not to mention, it would help her bid into society. This was the most coveted position at Harmony Prep!

"Well, I will have to look through the remaining applications, of course." Mrs. Mathison looked down at the large stack on her desk and then back at Bryna. "But I am sure you are a perfect fit. Our distinguished alumnus, Felicity Rose, will be heading the committee this year. I'll forward your application to her, and she will be in contact over the break."

"Thank you so much." Bryna stood and shook her teacher's hand.

"No. Thank you for all of your hard work."

She smiled brightly and then exited the room. Avery and Tara were seated in the hallway beside another cheerleader, Jemma.

"Glad that's all cleared away," Bryna said, clasping her hands behind her back. "Mrs. Mathison chose me to head the Pink Charity Benefit. Dream come true."

"Oh my God," Avery squealed.

"That's amazing!" Tara said.

"How could she have already picked you?" Jemma asked. "The applications were due yesterday. First round of interviews are supposed to be this afternoon."

Bryna shrugged. "Not my problem. Don't worry though. I'll save spaces for you all to be my assistants."

She brushed past the girls without a second thought. She was queen. Of course she was chair the committee. To think anyone else really had a shot was laughable.

She headed to the cheer room for practice after school. The other girls wouldn't get there until after they spoke with Mrs. Mathison, which would give Bryna time to speak with Coach Baker.

Bryna knocked on the door to the cheerleading coach's office. "You wanted to see me?"

"Yes, Bryna. How was your interview with Mrs. Mathison?"

"I got the lead spot for the Pink Charity Benefit," she said proudly.

"That's good to hear." Coach Baker ran her hand back through her blonde bob and smiled. "I just wanted to discuss with you something that was brought to my attention this past weekend. Please take a seat."

Bryna wasn't sure what this was about, but by the look on her coach's face, she wasn't going to like it. She plopped down across from Coach Baker and waited.

"It was unfortunate that you had to miss the game this past weekend. I recently heard that you weren't absent due to illness, however, and I wanted to see what you had to say about it." Coach Baker shifted uncomfortably. She was a petite woman who truly cared for the girls who cheered for her. She likely hated having this conversation more than Bryna.

Bryna's eyebrows rose. "What I have to say? I was in bed all night and could barely move."

Coach Baker sighed. "I want to believe you, Bryna. I was told that you weren't home all night, and you were, in fact, out on a date."

"What?" she gasped. "Who told you that?"

"Your brother," she said apologetically. "He said that you weren't at home when he got in. I haven't confirmed with your parents because I wanted to speak with you first."

Bryna swallowed her red-hot anger. "Pace is my *step*brother. My father is filming in New Zealand until

Christmas, and my mother is probably off somewhere, coked out and sleeping with one of her twenty-something cabana boys. Feel free to verify with them, but neither was home. Nor was Pace, and for once, he never came into my room."

Coach Baker shifted uncomfortably. "What about your stepmother?"

"I didn't see her all night." Here came the theatrics. Bryna put her hand over her mouth and swallowed as if she had to keep from crying. She breathed in heavily, shook her head, and then looked away. She couldn't believe this was happening to her. "You don't know what it's like at home right now, Coach Baker. I was sick in my room, all alone. Pace is throwing out wild accusations. I don't have a parental figure in the house anymore. I look up to you so much, Coach Baker, and knowing that you might believe this of me just makes it all worse."

"Bryna, I'm sorry. I know things have been rough with your home life lately. You've been so consistent all these years, and this was just a one-time miss, so we'll put the whole thing behind us. Let's just get to practice."

"Thank you, Coach Baker," Bryna said, wiping her eyes. "Can I just have a minute before I go out there?"

"Of course."

Coach Baker walked out of her office to herd the rest of the team, and Bryna pulled out her cell phone. Dropping the theatrics, she let her temper take over. *How dare Pace rat me out to my coach!* She wouldn't stand for this. He couldn't get away with it. She hoped he knew what he had gotten himself into because, from now on, this wasn't just fun and games. He had messed with her life, and he was going to pay.

She jotted out a text message to Pace.

Game on.

Bryna left practice in a hurry. She wanted to get home and prepare for her inevitable showdown with Pace once he got home from football practice.

On her way out of the building, she'd told Avery and Tara how Pace had lied to their coach. They couldn't believe that he would lie, let alone stoop to that level, but they were glad nothing bad had come of it. She wished she had someone to confide in about Jude, but she couldn't tell the girls that she hadn't actually been sick.

On her way home, her phone started ringing. She glanced down at the display. *Gates.* She sighed. This had been a long time coming. She clicked the Bluetooth feature.

"You have one minute before I hang up," she answered.

"I'm sorry. I miss you. I want to make it up to you."

Bryna rolled her eyes. "And how does Chloe feel about that?"

"Chloe and I aren't even together, Bri."

"You're not a couple, or you're not fucking?"

"Bryna," he sighed. "Come on. I'm making an effort here."

"Sidestepping the question isn't making an effort," she responded. She was still pissed about what she had walked into that night with Chloe and Gates. He shouldn't have blindsided her with that.

"We're not together, and we're not fucking either. All right?"

"Fine."

"You and I are the only people in each other's lives who know the real person behind the mask. You were there for me before my acting career exploded. Everyone else sees the movies, and you see the dick who you agreed to date even though he was a nobody."

Bryna laughed despite herself. "I would never date a nobody. I knew you would be huge."

"Would be huge?" he asked, laughing.

"We're not talking about your dick, Gates!"

"Fine. Fine. I'm just trying to make this right. I'll be gone through most of Christmas break, but I actually have an appearance scheduled for New Year's Eve in Los Angeles. If you aren't seeing anyone else, maybe you could be my date?"

She didn't know her plans for Christmas or New Year's. Her dad was supposed to be in town for both, as far as he had told her, and she usually dropped everything to spend as much time with him as possible. Also, she didn't know if, by the end of the month, she would have a hot New Year's date with Jude all lined up.

"I don't know. If nothing else comes up, then count me in. But just as a friend, Gates."

"Sounds like a vote of confidence, B. I invite you to the Chateau Marmont hotel for a posh New Year's exclusive, and you say, only if you don't find a better offer."

Bryna's heart rate picked up in excitement. "The Chateau Marmont? You are on the rise, aren't you?"

"Say you'll go with me."

"I stand by my answer."

Gates laughed. "If I didn't know better, I'd think you were seeing someone else."

"What is *that* supposed to mean?" she demanded.

"I know you, and you wouldn't be interested in some Harmony or Covenant trust fund baby. And with your extracurricular schedule, where would you find the time to meet someone new who could compete with me?"

Bryna shook her head in disbelief. This had been a relatively pleasant conversation up until that comment. Now, the anger that had momentarily dissolved was rearing its ugly head again.

"You're right. How could anyone ever compete with the ex-boyfriend I dumped for lying to me about sleeping with his costar? In fact, maybe you should just invite Chloe to the New Year's party."

"Oh, so there is someone."

"Stop fishing," she snapped.

Gates laughed lightly. "I'm not fishing. I have to get back. I hope I see you on New Year's, Bri."

"Bye, Gates." She hung up the phone with relief.

She felt like she was performing on a tightrope. Every footstep forward left her wobbling and in a more precarious position than the step before, but she couldn't turn around now. All she could do was keep walking down the unsteady rope and hope she would make it over to the other side without falling and breaking her neck.

FOURTEEN

"So, B," Pace said, leaning against the wall next to Bryna's locker, "you going to Jemma's house party this weekend? Her parents are out of town." He waggled his eyebrows up and down.

It took everything in her being not to throw the locker door into his smug face. Pace had never responded to her threatening text message earlier this week about interfering with Coach Baker. She was left waiting for another double-cross, and all she wanted to do was wrap her hands around his neck and throttle him. Except he might enjoy that. *Gross!*

"Isn't it enough that you harass me at home, Pace?" She stuffed her books into her bag.

"Hardly."

Bryna wrinkled her nose and slammed the locker shut.

"So, Jemma's party?" he asked again.

"No," she spat. "I'm not going to Jemma's party. I have better things to do."

Bryna started walking down the hall, but Pace fell into step beside her.

"What better things? Off with your mysterious stranger again? Are you going to tell me who he is? I know it's not Gates since he's out of town."

"I don't know what you're talking about," Bryna said.

Why does Pace have to latch on to this one thing? She couldn't let him find out about Jude. This was her secret to keep, and she didn't want Pace to have any leverage over her. He clearly wanted to ruin her life, and she shuddered to think what he would do if he found out.

"Don't you have class on the other side of campus?"

"I do," he agreed and then went right back to the other subject. "You should bring him to Jemma's party, so we can all meet him."

She stopped and glared at him. "I'm not going to Jemma's, and even if I were, I would be going solo."

"Because your date is too good for a Harmony party?"

"You're really stretching today, Pace."

She shook her head and vowed not to let him get under her skin. Just because he had told Coach Baker that she had been out on a date didn't mean that he knew it for a fact. *How could he know when he was at the football game and the only person who recognized me was a nobody, just some club promoter?*

Pace smiled the toothy grin that made her skin crawl. "I'm going to find out who he is, Bri."

"Good for you. Bye-bye now." She wagged her fingers at him and then stepped into English, her final class of the day.

Striding to the back of the room, she took her spot in between Avery and Tara. Avery immediately leaned over and started gabbing about something that had happened in her last class. Bryna couldn't concentrate on her nonsense right now.

Pace needed to stay out of her business, and she needed to start avoiding him at all costs. While her idiotic stepbrother was Valley trash, she wouldn't put it past him to resort to anything to discover who she was seeing. And if he found out, he would reveal her secret, and she couldn't risk Jude finding out that she was in high school. Not yet at least. She would have to undermine Pace before he could learn anything.

"Earth to queen bee," Tara said.

"What?" Bryna asked. She shook her head and turned to her friend. *What was she asking?*

"You have been way out of it lately."

Bryna shrugged. "I was plotting revenge."

"Revenge plots! Count us in," Avery squeaked.

"I'll call in reinforcements if necessary, but for now, I have it covered." At least she would when she figured out how to bring Pace down. The bastard would realize she was not to be messed with.

"Well, we were just asking about Jemma's party," Tara said.

"Yeah. Did you want to coordinate, so we arrive together?"

"Excuse me?" Bryna arched an eyebrow.

Avery and Tara exchanged hesitant glances.

"You can totally arrive last, Bri. We don't want to impose. We'll let you know what we're wearing, so you can make a grand entrance," Tara said quickly. She chewed on her thumbnail and turned to Avery for back up.

"Even better," Avery said, "we can find out what Jemma is wearing!"

"Plan our own sabotage!"

"Girls," Bryna said, holding up her hand, "I'm not going to Jemma's party."

"You're not?" they asked in unison.

"No."

"But her parents are out of town. I heard she even invited guys from Covenant," Avery told her.

Covenant was another local private school. They were rumored to have the hottest guys, and Harmony girls all flocked to them to find out if it was true. Bryna always thought that the rumor had been spread by people who couldn't get into Harmony.

"Who needs Covenant when I have all of Los Angeles to myself?"

Avery and Tara shared a confused look, and Bryna sighed dramatically.

"Max got me on the list at a completely exclusive new club. It's so outrageous that it doesn't even have a name right now. Everyone is just calling it X."

"X?" Tara asked.

"Like ecstasy?" Avery guessed.

Bryna laughed. "Let's hope that's just the warm-up round."

Both girls giggled.

"You truly are the queen, Bri," Avery fawned. Tara nodded enthusiastically.

"I know." She smiled with approval at her two subjects.

Her English teacher started up his lecture, and Bryna pulled out her phone. She typed out a text message to get her plan set in motion.

Max, get me on the list for X on Saturday night.

FIFTEEN

"YOU PLANNED THIS WHOLE THING, didn't you?" Pace asked, barging into her room.

"That's it. I'm going to get a deadbolt installed on my bedroom door. I don't even know how you got through that lock!" Bryna cried.

Pace produced a credit card. "Don't they teach you spoiled rich kids anything?"

"Clearly not," she drawled sarcastically. "Now, get the fuck out of my room."

"You think this is all a game? Is that what your fucking text meant?" he demanded.

"Oh, so you did read it."

She crossed her arms and sank into her hip. At least she was finally getting through to him. Even if she couldn't keep him out of her fucking room.

"Don't fuck with me, Bri. My mom is downstairs right now. She just told me that she hasn't seen me enough, and suddenly, me and the twins are supposed to have a family night." Pace accusingly glared at Bryna.

Bryna shrugged innocently. "I can't help what your mom wants you to do."

"And it all happens on the same night as the biggest house party of the year. It's not a fucking coincidence!"

Her grin only widened. "Coincidences happen all the time, Pace."

"Is this just a pathetic attempt to get back at me for talking to your cheer coach?' he demanded. He looked ready to blow a gasket. "Or are you just pissed because you're not queen of Harmony anymore?"

"If I'm not queen, then why am I leaving to go to X while you're staying here to play board games?" she asked with a triumphant smile.

"You think you're going to leave this house and go to some ecstasy party while I'm stuck here?" Pace crossed his arms and stood in her way. A bulldozer could have been less formidable. "Fuck no."

"That's cute." She fluttered her fingers at him, trying to remain nonplussed. "But I'm not part of whatever family gathering you have planned for tonight. As far as I'm concerned, you're just some total creeper living in my house, so get the fuck out of my way."

"Or else what?" he asked.

"Or else I'll scream. Try to explain that one." She sent him a seething stare.

He glared back at her, but then he stepped out of the way. "I'm going to get you for this."

"Whatever, Pace."

Bryna strode out of her room and down the giant staircase. Her stepmother was standing at the bottom of the stairs. She smiled and waved Bryna over.

"Bryna, dear, have you seen where Pace ran off to? He was supposed to grab a sweater and then be right down. The twins just picked out a movie."

"Yes. He's in my room, jerking off."

Celia jolted at the coarse phrasing. "He's…what?"

"You'll have to see for yourself."

"I'll check on him in a minute," she said uncertainly.

Celia focused back on Bryna. She surveyed Bryna up and down in her tight strapless red dress and mile-high strappy fuck-me boots. Her long blonde hair was pulled over one shoulder, and her makeup was dark, smoky, and seductive. She was a walking sexpot.

"You don't look like you're staying in for family night in that outfit." Celia looked like she wanted to say "young lady" at the end of the sentence, but somehow managed to restrain herself.

"That's because I'm not," Bryna said, grabbing her black leather moto jacket off of a hook and brushing past her stepmom.

"I know you don't always like what I have to say, Bryna, but I think if you go out in that outfit you're going to give boys the wrong idea."

Bryna sighed and then looked at her stepmom with fake sympathy. "First off, I'm not attracting *boys*, and second, I think I'm giving them exactly the right idea."

She wrenched open the front door and left her stepmom standing there in shock. She was sure that Celia wanted to say something more, but thankfully Bryna had stunned her into silence. She didn't need to hear anymore about what kind of guys her body would attract. She was already well aware, and her stepmother was an idiot if she thought that Bryna didn't already know what to do with her body.

A limo was waiting for her in the private circle drive in front of her parents' mansion. When she stepped inside, Avery and Tara were already in the limo.

They both gasped when they saw her.

"You look so fucking hot!" Avery cried.

"Seriously, no guy will be able to resist you," Tara agreed.

"I just wish we knew who the guy was who has stolen you away," Avery said excitedly. She nudged Bryna in the side and exchanged an eager look with Tara.

"Yeah, we've been waiting for you to spill," Tara said.

"What?" Bryna asked, reaching for the champagne to cover her shock.

She hadn't told anyone that she was seeing someone new. Ever since she and Gates had officially broken up, she had been playing up the single life at school, so no one would suspect. Somehow, the rumor was flying around anyway. She suspected Pace's treachery.

"Oh, come on. We know you're dating someone. Who is it?" Avery asked. "Is it a Covenant guy? Is that why we're avoiding Jemma's party? You're not ready to be seen together yet?"

Bryna took a sip of the champagne and let the bubbly cool her temper. She needed to squash these rumors and fast. "We're not going to the party because Max got us on the list at X. I don't even know why I have to explain this. Plus, I'd never downgrade to a Covenant guy. Don't insult me."

"We didn't—"

"That's not what we—"

"Save it," Bri said, holding up her hand. "Let's toast to X and sweet, sweet revenge tonight."

The girls clinked their glasses together and then tossed their drinks back. By the time they got through traffic, they were well into their second bottle of champagne and feeling the buzz. They exited the limo in front of a blank gray building. To anyone else passing by, it just looked like a warehouse, but Bryna knew it was the scandalous nightclub X. The best places in town had no signs and no advertisement. X was no exception. Only the hottest, most select group of people knew this place existed.

Bryna and her friends sauntered right up to the man with the clipboard at the door and were whisked inside within seconds. She silently thanked Max for getting them on the list.

The room was dark with red lighting shining through divided sheer curtains. Gorgeous girls in red-and-black lingerie danced on pedestals. A hip-hop beat thumped loudly in the background. Couples were already making out on the dance floor or fondling each other in the mostly obscure corners. It was raunchy and enticing and everything she wanted in one place. It was not as sophisticated as Allure and not as high school as Luxe.

The girls were escorted to a booth with bottle service. A set of curtains separated them from some hot businessmen. Avery was already making eyes at one of them through the divider. The man slid between the curtains and asked her to dance while Bryna popped open another bottle of Dom.

A gorgeous man glanced her way, and she knew without even offering him a smile that he would come over. Tonight was one to indulge, and while he was undeniably attractive, she didn't want to indulge *too* much. She would take her excess with alcohol and drugs, not with her other vices. She and Jude hadn't drawn any exclusivity lines, but she didn't want to jeopardize the possibility by fucking around with some other guy.

"Dance?" the man asked, nodding his head toward the floor where Avery had just disappeared.

Bryna considered his offer. She promised herself that she would be careful. Dancing wouldn't cause any harm. She had no intention of going further. Plus, she couldn't come out to the hottest nightclub and not get lost in the music for a little while. She was only young once.

"Sure. Why not?" She gave him an irresistible smile and then downed her full glass of champagne.

He grabbed her hand and pulled her away from the booth. Tara followed shortly afterward with another guy from a nearby table. They danced through three songs beside Avery and Tara. Then, Bryna left to get another drink. She grabbed her phone as she poured herself a flute of champagne. She stopped with the drink halfway to her lips when she realized she had missed two calls from Jude.

"Fuck!"

She wasn't going to be able to hear a fucking thing in the club. Knocking back the drink, she found somewhere quiet and called him back.

"Hey, Bri."

"Hey!" she called over the noise. "Sorry I missed you. What's up?"

"I got back into the city, and already, my flight out is delayed until the morning due to horrible East Coast weather, which means that I'm free for the night. I'd like to spend it with you."

Bryna contemplated what to do. There was no way that Avery and Tara could know that Jude was the guy she had been seeing, and she simply couldn't introduce Jude to her high school friends. Both things were bound to end up in disaster. Yet she couldn't exactly abandon Avery and Tara after hyping up X all week. They would be suspicious about why she was leaving, and then they would think she really was jetting off to see her mysterious boyfriend.

She bit her lip and tried to figure a solution to the puzzle. She needed to figure out a way to make this all work without getting caught in the crossfire.

An idea popped into her head, and she smiled devilishly. " Want to play a game?"

He chuckled seductively. "I'm listening."

"When we get off the line, I'll text you the address of the nightclub where I am, and I'll make sure your name is on the list. I've suddenly forgotten who you are. So, come and find a hot blonde in a red dress and seduce her. She might go home with you—if you're lucky."

SIXTEEN

A FEW MINUTES LATER, Jude had the address to X, and his name was on the list. Bryna occupied herself with dancing, switching up partners to keep any one guy from monopolizing her time. She was giddy and jittery at the same time.

Jude was coming here.

She couldn't suppress the fluttering in her stomach at the prospect of seeing him in such a way. Not to mention the nerves knowing that she could get caught with him, knowing that anything could go wrong. It was dangerous and thus, unbelievably enticing.

At one point while they were on the dance floor, Tara disappeared. Avery claimed Tara just had to use the restroom, but the guy she had been with was gone too. It took her twenty minutes to surface, and she looked both disheveled and smug. Bryna just laughed at her friend's poor excuse and moved her hips to the beat of the music.

She had just started another dance with the businessman from next to their booth when she felt eyes on her. It was inexplicable with hundreds of people in the room, but there it was. Someone was watching her. She smiled as if she were on display and started grinding against the stranger.

The feeling grew stronger, but Jude never surfaced. She turned around and threw her arms around the guy in front of her. Her eyes skimmed the dark room to try to figure out where he could be hiding. She didn't know why he was watching when he could be partaking.

Well, she would have to fight dirty to get him to play. Bryna slid her hand across the guy's neck, down his chest, and to the waistline of his pants. She swirled her hips in slow circles as she faced away from him once more. She leaned against him and rolled her body back against his. He forcefully gripped her hips in his hands. His head dropped down and nuzzled her neck. She played along, tilting her head back and closing her eyes.

Then, he took it a step further and started kissing against her sensitive skin. Before she could even react to the change, she was wrenched forward, away from the guy, and lips were covering her own. These lips she most definitely recognized.

Her heart thrummed to the beat of the music, but all she could feel was the need rolling off of Jude. She greedily kissed him back. God, she had missed him. It had only been a week, but it had felt like forever.

She completely forgot where she was or what she was doing when the idiot businessman decided to butt in.

"Hey, man, we were dancing."

Jude broke away from her, gave the guy the best eat-shit-and-die look she had ever seen, and then escorted her away. She didn't even argue or look back at her friends, who had probably just witnessed what happened.

Before Bryna and Jude even reached the edge of the dance floor, his lips were on hers again. She could barely breathe with all the bodies pressed so tightly around them.

"I think my seduction went from zero to sixty in about two point four seconds," he said.

"Well, at least you have good taste. I love a Bugatti."

"Very good taste," he said, drawing her even closer. "But who said other guys could kiss you?"

Bryna arched an eyebrow. "No one has told me otherwise."

"Consider yourself told."

A thrill ran through her body. "No kisses from anyone else then," she agreed. A thrill ran through her. "What about touching?" She ran her hand down his pants and along the length of his cock.

"I'll show you just what you can do with that," he growled.

She tightened her hand around him and smiled. "Show me."

He smirked defiantly and pulled her off the dance floor.

She pointed in the opposite direction as she moved in close to talk to him. "I have a booth—"

"I'm seducing you, remember?"

He grabbed her ass and then pressed her in front of him. They walked away from the main dance floor and up to a bouncer standing watch over a dark hallway. Jude passed the guy a wad of cash and nodded his head. The velvet rope disappeared, and she was whisked down the hallway.

"How did you know about this?" she whispered as she crossed the threshold into a red-lit room.

Couches lined the walls, and a circular divan rested against the back wall. It looked like an empty sex club. She had heard of clubs in the city having these private rooms. She had never been to one before, but Gates had called them dungeons. Some were to watch, and some were to play. This one definitely looked like play.

"Work."

Bryna's eyes bulged at that. She didn't often show her surprise, but had Jude just admitted to being involved in dungeons?

He chuckled softly at the shock on her face and kissed her. "Not me in particular, but I have...coworkers who get involved. I take care of their interests."

"Well, if that wasn't as vague as you could possibly be," she said. "Sounds like you're a pimp."

He laughed. "Some days, it feels like that."

"So, you've been here before then?"

"Enough questions," he demanded.

She clamped her mouth shut and tried to rid herself of all the burning questions she had for him. It wasn't as if she didn't have any secrets.

He walked her backward until her boots were touching the divan, slid the hem of her dress up, and smiled smugly when he found her without panties on.

"Like what you see?" she whispered.

"I said no more questions," he said with a twinkle in his eye. Then, he roughly pushed her onto the divan. "Lie back."

She did as instructed and stared up at the ceiling. He toed her legs farther apart until she was spread wide for his viewing pleasure. Her core pulsed in anticipation. God, she couldn't wait for his dick. She would stay up at night, thinking about the way he used it to bring her over the edge, and inevitably, she would then bring herself there, too.

He dropped to his knees before her, and she sat up in surprise. He licked his lips as he stared into her eyes.

"I said, lie back," he said sternly.

Bryna dropped back onto the cushion. Jude's lips started where the cuff of her boot covered her knee, and then he kissed his way up to her inner thigh. His tongue flicked along her clit, causing her entire body to jerk. She dug her fingers into the cushion as he went to work, slowly licking and sucking.

She closed her eyes and arched her back at the sudden assault. His arm forced her body back down, and when he had her restrained, he used his other hand to insert two fingers deep inside her.

If this was his idea of seduction, she was a lost cause. She wasn't used to being completely out of control, and her body was already begging him to let her come.

He tasted and indulged in her until she was writhing against his restraint. His fingers pressed into the smooth wet skin, curved up inside her, and brushed against her inner wall. She tightened until she thought she was going to burst before finally climaxing. Her walls contracted around his fingers as he slid out. She was left panting.

Bryna started to close her legs, but he tapped them with his fingers twice. She looked up at him questioningly. Her body was still pulsing, and she could barely focus.

He twirled his finger in a circle in the air. "Turn over."

She started to stand up, but he grasped her hips in his hands and flipped her over with ease. Her elbows supported her while her bare ass was in the air for his viewing pleasure.

"Mmm," he groaned. He ran his finger from her pussy to her asshole.

Her body was still so sensitive, and the unexpected touch jolted her.

He pulled back and rested his hand on her ass. "Hmm. Did you like that?"

"I…" She cleared her throat. "I'm not sure."

She had never had any back door action. She'd had guys try to convince her, and while she had been intrigued by it, she had never followed through.

"Would you like to try?" he asked, sliding his hand up her back in a soothing motion.

Her body quivered lightly as he repeated the motion, the languid movement getting her used to him touching her again.

His touch made her feel good, and if he was asking, then he surely knew what he was doing. She would trust him to make her comfortable.

"Yes," she whispered.

"Hmm?" he asked.

He pressed his finger against her, and she tightened in response.

"Are you sure?"

She was getting wetter the longer she rested on her knees before him, allowing him to touch and tempt her body. He was all she wanted, however he was willing to give himself to her.

"I'll do whatever you want," she said, offering up the control he had already taken.

"I think I'll have to warm you up to that," he said.

The sound of his pants swishing to the floor was all the warning she was given before his dick buried deep inside her pussy. She gasped as he filled her. The force of the movement shoved her forward across the divan, and her already hypersensitive body responded.

Is this his idea of warming me up? She had already come once.

He continued to thrust into her, and she balanced precariously on all fours. Her mind went fuzzy, and in that moment, all she could feel was Jude. She was getting closer, and still Jude didn't stop. He reached around her body and started stroking her clit. She bucked against him, but he kept up the movement.

It was almost too much at once. Jude pounded into her. Her hair cascaded over her shoulders and into her face. Everything was spinning. She could barely breathe as she tried to keep up with his thrusts. Her whole body felt like it was on fire.

As if he knew that she was teetering on the edge, Jude slowed his movements, completely filling her to the hilt one more time, and then removed his dick. Bryna immediately felt a loss in his absence. She had been so close. She squirmed back and forth, hoping to draw him back in, but he just playfully smacked her ass.

"Stay still, or your ass will be pink by the time I'm done with you."

Bryna swallowed, and her body hummed at his words. *Holy shit, that was hot!*

She glanced backward and saw Jude walking across the room. He pushed open a small sliding door that she hadn't even noticed in the dim lighting. He picked something off of a shelf and then turned back toward her. She quickly righted herself. She couldn't believe this was going to happen...that she was going to do this. But she wanted to take whatever he would give her.

A loud thwack sounded in the room as Jude smacked her ass ten times harder than the first time. She yelped out loud.

"That's for peeking."

His hand landed on the other cheek just as hard. She cried out again.

"And that's just because I like how wet your pussy gets when I spank you."

His left hand touched her back and then gently rubbed her ass. Then, his finger, slick with lube, slowly eased into her ass. "Relax," he murmured soothingly.

She released all the tension in her body, and he slid in further. She swallowed hard and tried to stay calm. Clenching or freaking out would only make this harder. He worked his fingers in and out until she was ready for him, and then he replaced them with the tip of his dick.

He entered her slowly. Her body protested, but he just muttered soft words of encouragement, "It's okay. You're going to like it."

She breathed in and out and then nodded her head, giving him permission to keep going.

He slipped the head in, and her body seemed to accept what was happening. She felt so full but in a completely different way. Pain mixed with pleasure as he retreated and then started up a gentle motion back inside her.

She could tell that Jude was holding back as he eased her into the play. She could practically feel him quivering with desire. He had worked her into such a frenzy as he fucked her, and now, he was claiming her like no one else ever had.

Just that thought alone sent her eyes rolling into the back of her head. This wasn't so bad. It was actually...really good. She liked the way it made her pussy ache for his touch and the way she felt kind of dirty for trying something she had never done before. But most of all, she loved how it affected Jude.

He wanted her bent over the divan, pussy thoroughly worked with her ass in the air, filled up to the brim with his cock. She clenched around him, and he started to lose control, jerking against her and tightening his grip on her hips.

"Jude, I'm going to come," she cried. "Make me come."

"Fuck," he groaned.

He drove into her again, and she couldn't hold out any longer. They released together in an earth-shattering explosion. Her hands gave out beneath her, and she slipped forward with her face landing in the pillows. Her screams were muffled as she cried out in ecstasy.

Maybe that was the reason the club was called X.

SEVENTEEN

BRYNA WAS GLAD THAT SCHOOL WAS OUT for Christmas break. On Monday morning, she didn't have to explain to anyone where she had gone on Saturday night or what had happened. She would rather leave it all up to speculation than face Avery's and Tara's questioning stares. They had already sent her enough texts, asking her about the guy she had disappeared with that night. She was glad she didn't have to lie to their faces.

After getting good use out of the back room, she and Jude had returned to his apartment. She couldn't get over their connection and the physical chemistry that ignited a room when they were together. She hadn't gotten much sleep Saturday night, but the sex wasn't the part that had her mind running a million miles a minute after he'd left the next morning to catch his flight. It was the fact that he would have a full week off for Christmas, and he wanted to spend every one of those days with *her*.

She had told him that she would have to check her schedule. Her dad was supposed to come home soon, so it would be a little harder to sneak around—though not by much. Also, she wasn't sure how she would get away with leaving on Christmas Day. But she would make it work. This would be one of the few times that she would get this much of Jude's undivided attention, and she was going to take it.

It was still a couple days away, so she had time to figure it all out.

She had to force herself to stop thinking about that as she headed to The Blvd, a restaurant at the Beverly Wilshire, to meet with the Pink Charity Benefit coordinator, Felicity Rose.

Bryna had done some research on her to prepare for this meeting. Felicity had graduated top of her class from Harmony over a decade ago and received a degree in anthropology from Stanford. Now, she chaired the Foundation for Children in Need, was President of the L.A. Society Committee, and volunteered at the Emma Allgood Institute for the homeless—all on top of heading the Pink Charity Benefit for Harmony.

This was just the kind of woman Bryna needed to emulate. She was a real role model, unlike the other women in her life. Thankfully, Bryna's father would be home from filming soon, and she wouldn't have to deal with her evil witch of a stepmother. Her father would handle that situation for her. Maybe then things could get back to normal.

Bryna valeted her Aston Martin and then entered the restaurant. "Reservation for Felicity Rose," she told the hostess.

"Right this way."

The hostess walked her over to a perfectly put-together woman. Felicity had dark blonde hair pulled back tight off of her face. She was in a square-cut dress with a Chanel blazer that Bryna had been coveting this season. At least the woman had taste even if she looked like a stuck-up bitch.

"Mrs. Rose," Bryna said with a huge smile on her face. "So nice to finally meet you."

"Please calm me Felicity. You must be Bryna."

"That's me."

"Why don't you take a seat?" Felicity offered.

"Thank you." Bryna sat demurely in the seat across from Felicity.

Felicity took the time to carefully unfold her napkin and lay it across her lap. She then adjusted the silverware into order and took a small sip of her Pellegrino. "I reviewed your file. To be honest, I was a bit surprised Mrs. Mathison sent you over."

Bryna bristled at the comment. Who the hell did she think could replace her? There was no one else at Harmony for this job. No one else could compare that was for sure. "Why is that?"

"I didn't really expect a...*cheerleader,*" she said, the last word coming out as if she had just sucked on a lemon. "Then, there's your affiliation with this Gates Hartman."

Where the hell is this coming from? It shouldn't matter that she was a cheerleader if she was smart, hard working, and motivated to succeed. That was what she had always told herself at least. *And anyway, what the hell does Gates have to do with anything?*

"And the unfortunate situation with your parents..." Felicity continued.

"Is all of that in my file?" Bryna asked dryly.

She couldn't fucking believe Felicity was airing out everything in her life, all because of a charity benefit application. So, Bryna's life wasn't actually picture-perfect. Well, she already fucking knew that.

All she wanted to do was tell this woman to fuck off, but she was pretty sure she would lose her position. And she wasn't going to lose her hard earned spot because a has-been was trying to knock her down a few notches.

"I did a little research of my own," Felicity said cheekily.

"By all means, be sure to run a background check on a seventeen-year-old high school student."

Felicity stared back at her, all prim and proper. "That won't be necessary."

"Wonderful. Can I be clear with you as to why I applied for this position in the first place?" Bryna didn't wait for her to answer. She didn't care what the bitch had to say. She had the wrong impression about her, and Bryna wouldn't let it stand. "This is my senior year at Harmony. I'm currently ranked fifth in my class. I run the National Distinguished Students Association, all while acting as captain of the cheerleading squad. I *work* for the things in my life, something I think you can understand. The Pink Charity Benefit is the most extensive event for Harmony every year, and I want to be a part of something that contributes so much to the community. Please allow me to work just as hard to give back."

"Hmm."

Apparently, that was all the response Bryna was going to get. The waiter walked over, and Felicity glanced down at her menu.

"I'll have the raspberry spinach salad. No dressing."

As Bryna read the menu, her phone started ringing. She silently cursed its bad timing. She turned the ringer off and saw that her dad was calling. "I'm sorry. I have to take this."

Felicity pursed her lips.

"It's my dad calling from New Zealand. It must be important. I'll have the same salad," she said before hopping up and answering her phone.

"Dad!"

"Hey, sweetheart! How's daddy's little girl?"

"Not too little anymore. I'm at a meeting with this year's Pink Charity coordinator. I'm heading the event."

"Very grown-up indeed. Congratulations!"

"Thank you! How is New Zealand?" she gushed.

"New Zealand is beautiful. I wish you could come out here and visit," he said thoughtfully.

"Well, I'd love to, but I won't have to," she told him cheerfully. "You'll be coming home soon. I cannot wait to have you back in the house."

There was a long pause on the line before her dad sighed. "That's why I called, sweetheart. The film has been pushed back and delayed. We've just increased the budget by another twenty million dollars, and we're shooting through Christmas."

Bryna's stomach dropped. No. No, he couldn't do this. He couldn't leave her alone with these people any longer. He was supposed to be back for Christmas. They were supposed to spend the holidays together. It was tradition. He couldn't do this to her.

"Dad," she whispered. Her voice sounded desperate. She *was* desperate. "Please."

"Bryna, I know. I want to come home, but I have to work."

"Work comes first," she said bitterly.

"You know how the business is." He sounded so blasé she felt sick.

"I do." She sagged at the words. She did understand the business.

She had long lived with an absentee father and a distant mother. As much as she had wanted it to work with them, they hadn't been around enough for either of them to try in their relationship. But that hadn't made it okay for him to marry someone else and *leave* her with Celia and her disgusting spawn while he was away. Things had only gotten they were worse since Celia arrived.

"Once I'm finished with this film, we'll fly out to Paris, and you can get lost in your favorite boutiques."

"Just the two of us?" she pleaded.

"You and me, kiddo. Just like old times."

Somehow, she just didn't believe him.

"Okay, Dad, sounds good." She knew it would never happen.

"Love you, baby girl. I'll let you know when we're wrapping up."

"Bye," she said wistfully.

She hung up the phone and tightly held it in her hand. The entire holiday, she was going to be trapped with Celia, Pace, and the twins. No father to intervene with the madness. No father to reconcile the huge gap that had divided the house in his absence. No father to be…a father. Just a faraway director. No father at all.

Bryna squared her shoulders and walked back to the table. "My apologies. My father had to inform me of his last-minute change in plans. He'll be staying in New Zealand for the holiday season. Sorry about the interruption. It won't happen again."

"Good," Felicity said. She didn't even react to Bryna's statement about her father. "So, let's get started."

"Just like that?" Bryna asked.

After the third degree Felicity put me through, she's going to hand over the position?

"Do you no longer want to lead the committee?"

"Of course I do," Bryna said emphatically.

"I thought so. You seem to work hard and clearly don't back down from a challenge," Felicity said with a quirked eyebrow. *So, it all was a test.* "I think we can make this partnership succeed, if you're up for it."

"I'm up for anything."

EIGHTEEN

WITH BRYNA'S FATHER OUT OF TOWN FOR CHRISTMAS, she found the excuse she needed to disappear for a week.

"You're sure that you're going to be gone the entire Christmas?" Celia asked. "We won't even see you on Christmas day?"

Bryna sighed. She didn't want to look too sympathetic or Celia wouldn't buy it. "Look I just don't get to spend any quality time with my mother, and since dad is going to be gone the whole time, it seemed like a perfect opportunity. No reason to split time between the house if he isn't going to be here"

Celia pursed her lips. "Well, of course I want you to have quality time with your mother, but I will miss you dearly, honey. The whole house will miss you."

"I'm sure."

Bryna resisted the urge to roll her eyes. She certainly wouldn't miss her overbearing stepmother or Pace. Especially Pace.

He hadn't spoken to her since the incident with Jemma's party, which was fine by her. She didn't ever want to talk to him again if she could help it. She knew that the silent treatment was probably too good to be true. She was sure he was plotting something behind his silence. He wasn't giving up yet.

It would be nice to get away from the cold shoulder and constant seething.

So, once her Louis Vuitton luggage was packed, she hightailed it out of the house.

About an hour later, after sitting through hellish traffic, she parked her car at Jude's apartment. Jude let her inside when she showed up at his front door. He took her bags from her, set them down by the coffee table, and then scooped her up in his arms.

"I missed you," he said into her hair.

She closed her eyes and tightened her grip around his neck. "I missed you, too."

"Are you all ready to go?"

"Go where?" she asked, looking around the apartment.

"You didn't think I'd get you all to myself for a week and keep you cooped up in my apartment, did you?"

Well, yeah. She kind of had thought that. It had sounded pretty wonderful. No drama for a whole week. Just Jude.

"I think you'll like what I have in mind," he said with a wink.

She arched an eyebrow but didn't argue. As long as she was with him, then she knew she was going to like whatever he had planned.

Jude had a car waiting for them downstairs, and the driver placed her bags in the trunk. A bottle of champagne chilled in a silver bucket. Jude popped the top and poured them each a glass of the sparkling bubbly.

"To new beginnings," he said, raising his glass.

She clinked her flute against his and then took a sip. "Is this your new beginning?"

He smirked in an unbelievably charming way. "You're my new beginning, Bri."

She didn't know what to say to something so sweet. Guys weren't normally like this. They didn't really get her or know how to treat her. They were just silly boys. With Jude, it was different. She could spend all day wrapped in his arms and feel completely content. Nothing else had ever been like that. She was always so antsy, ready to do something else, anxious to get moving, scheming away in her head. Jude quieted all the noise and let her be.

About half an hour later, they were pulling off of Interstate 10, long before reaching the Santa Monica coastline.

Bryna glanced over at Jude in confusion. *Where the hell are they going?*

When the small Santa Monica Airport came into view, she was even more confused, not to mention curious. The car drove around and deposited them outside of a large hangar.

Bryna gaped. "What is going on?"

Jude looked smug. "Surprise."

"Surprise...what?"

The driver opened up her door, and she got out of the car. She was oscillating between shock and excitement.

"Seriously. What is going on?" she asked, as Jude hopped out behind her. He wrapped his arm around her waist and placed a kiss on her temple.

"You asked what was next—a private plane and a trip to Saint Barts."

She whipped around in his grip. "Tell me you're joking."

"I'm not joking."

Her hand flew to her mouth before she could even try for cool, calm, and collected. Jude was taking her on a private plane to spend the week of Christmas in St. Barts. Shock was definitely winning out.

"You said you take your passport with you everywhere."

She nodded softly at this. A man who had actually listened and remembered what she had said. She had counted on her own father to come home for Christmas, and he had let her down. Here was Jude, who had cared enough to go out of his way to plan this just for her. She was beyond shocked. She was completely floored and enamored.

"I take it you like it?"

She shook her head and then cracked up laughing. "Oh my God, I can't believe we're going away together."

He leaned down and kissed her hard on the lips. "I said it was a new beginning."

"You did. There's only one problem," she told him.

"What's that?"

"I didn't bring a swimsuit."

His eyes traveled the length of her body. "Where we're going, I don't think you'll need one."

She laughed again and gave him that one. She would absolutely need a swimsuit if she was going to be tucked away at a beach resort all break, but she liked his implication.

One thing was very clear. This was going to be the best Christmas *ever.*

The private plane had an interior cabin fitted with a plush cream leather sofa, two matching chairs, and a mounted big screen television.

A private attendant in a short blue uniform smiled at them upon their arrival. "Please make yourself comfortable. I'll be in the galley. Let me know if you need anything. We'll be taking off shortly," she said before disappearing.

Bryna took a seat in one of the chairs and checked her cell phone. She had two missed calls and a text message from Celia. *Ugh!*

> *Bryna, please let me know when you make it to your mother's safely. Have a great Christmas. We'll miss you! Also, Pace says to have a great time.*

She groaned at the message. *What an overbearing and insufferable human being!* She was obviously leaving to go see her mom to get away from her stepfamily. Even if it was all a ruse so that she could go away with Jude, they didn't have to keep messaging her. *Doesn't my stepmother get that?*

And Pace! She was fairly certain he had told his mother to send that shit just to irritate her. She wasn't going to let it bother her. She was on a private jet with Jude, about to leave for St. Barts. Nothing was going to get in her way.

> *Just got here. All safe. Tell Pace to have fun with Jemma over break.*

A confident smile played on her features. If his mother was overbearing with her, then she would surely be that way with Pace. Bryna couldn't wait for all the questions to be hurled his way.

She looked up from the screen and into Jude's questioning eyes. She shrugged and stuffed the phone into the pocket of her black skinny jeans. She figured it was Christmas, so it would be safe to actually mention parents without sounding like she was still living at home. "Just my stepmother asking about Christmas…again."

Jude nodded. "I see, and you don't want to spend the holiday with them?"

"No," she answered immediately. "I want to spend the holiday with you. Only you."

"Good. I want nothing else."

She smiled as she stood and sauntered over to where he was sitting on the couch, and then she straddled him. Her fingers threaded into his hair, and she dropped her mouth down onto his. This was the most romantic and amazing thing anyone had ever done for her, and all she wanted to do was show her gratitude.

The kiss heated as his hands slid down her sides and around to grab her ass. She started grinding her hips against him as if she were giving him a lap dance right then and there. She groaned into his mouth and then dragged his bottom lip through her teeth.

His hands continued to explore her body, sliding under her black tank top and blue blazer, climbing up her spine, and then moving around to her full breasts. Her whole body responded to the way he cupped and massaged her tits. One finger dipped inside the cup and flicked her nipple, causing her to arch against him.

"Fuck," he moaned.

Then, he was hoisting her off of him and throwing her down on the couch. Her legs wrapped around his waist as he leaned over her. He kissed his way up her neck as his pelvis thrust against her in the most inviting way. God, she wanted to rip his clothes off.

A soft cough sounded from the back of the plane, and instantly, they both seemed to remember exactly where they were. The plane hadn't even taken off. They hadn't even left the city. They would have an audience until they were twenty thousand feet up.

Jude quickly straightened and helped Bryna into a sitting position as the attendant gave them flight instructions. Takeoff was a breeze. Soon, they were flying high on what Jude informed her was a nearly eight-hour flight from Los Angeles. Since it was a private plane, they would get there without any stops, but it would still be the next morning before they arrived.

After getting good use out of the cabin and effectively joining the mile high club, Bryna lay in Jude's lap with a content sigh.

"This is the life," she murmured drowsily.

He gently stroked her hair back, and she closed her eyes at the soothing motion.

"It's one I'm glad you're in."

She yawned as she said, "Me...too."

"Why don't you try to sleep? I have some work I need to get done anyway."

"What are you working on?" she asked, peeking up at him.

He gave her *the* look, the one she had come to associate with things he didn't want to talk about. She never pushed it. He would tell her when he was ready. Just like she would tell him that she was seventeen...as soon as she wasn't seventeen anymore. *God, why do I have to have a July birthday?*

"Nothing. Just go to sleep. When you wake up, we'll be in paradise."

She smiled up at him and let the issue slide. All she could think about as she drifted off to sleep to the sound of him clicking away on his laptop was how much she wished she could tell him everything about her.

One day, she wouldn't have to hide from him the things everyone else already knew about her, but she didn't think she would be able to share things he only knew about her heart with anyone else. Despite the secrets piled up between them, she felt she was utterly and unequivocally falling for this mysterious man.

NINETEEN

THEY TOUCHED DOWN at the tiny St. Barts airport at around two in the morning. Jude had a car waiting to take them away, and Bryna snuggled up against him in the backseat as they drove the short distance to their destination.

Their illuminated beach house revealed an enormous red-roofed villa right on the water. Even in the dark, it looked like something she couldn't have even dreamed up. The villa itself had six bedrooms and seven baths with a crystal-clear rectangular pool, a covered cabana, and the most spectacular view of the ocean.

Jude deposited their bags in a massive master bedroom complete with a full sitting room, a bed large enough to comfortably sleep a half dozen, and a walk-in closet larger than her one at home. The bathroom had a Jacuzzi tub that she could swim in with a window overlooking the pool.

All in all, Jude had been right. It was paradise.

The next morning, Bryna woke up to the sun rising over the ocean. After exploring the villa in the daylight, they drove into town to get breakfast. Bryna purchased a couple of new bathing suits at a boutique nearby even though Jude had kept whispering in her ear that he was just going to take them off. Then they returned to the villa and spent the rest of the afternoon lounging in the sun and swimming in the pool.

They had been enjoying their days by the water and their nights in the bedroom so much that Bryna was surprised when she woke up on Thursday to realize that Christmas was already here. Living in Los Angeles, she had never had a white Christmas unless her family vacationed in Paris or New York City. But with highs in the mid-eighties and not a cloud in the sky, Christmas in St. Barts felt even more surreal.

Or maybe it was that she wouldn't see any of her family. She tried not to let that fact bum her out, but she had this unexpected feeling of unease as soon as she woke up. She hadn't heard from her mother in months. Her father was busy in New Zealand. *Who knows if I'll even hear from him today?* She had no brothers and sisters, and she refused to even consider her stepfamily as relatives she should be missing on this holiday. Even though people constantly surrounded her, she felt very...alone.

Maybe she should be used to it. After all, it wasn't like this was some new thing. Her father loved her, but he spent more time working than he ever did with her. She had been closer to her mother when she was younger, but as she grew up, her mother had become more and more distant. It was hard not to blame that on herself rather than on the fact that her parents' marriage had come apart at the seams.

So, what's different?

Jude.

For the first time in a long time, she felt completely wanted. He treated her right, cared about her, and gave her the affection that she had been lacking in her life. With everyone else, she could wear her confidence on her sleeve. She didn't need friends or family or a boyfriend. She was strong, brilliant, and ready to take over the world. But Jude disarmed her, and when she was with him, she realized how alone she had always felt before this.

At that thought, she rolled over to wrap her arms around Jude, but she realized that his side of the bed was empty—again. A moment of panic hit her when she thought about how he had left her that first night they had been together, but then she recovered. They were on an island in the Caribbean. *Where could he possibly go?*

"Jude?" she called, walking out of the bedroom in nothing but a sexy red baby doll.

She padded into the living room and heard the sound of his voice coming from the kitchen. She almost entered but stopped when she realized he was on the phone.

"No, I'm not going to be over today." There was a short pause. "I know what you want, but I'm away on business. I'm not even getting back until right before New Year's."

Hmm. She wondered who he was talking to. She hadn't expected him to tell anyone that he was away with her, but it kind of hurt that he was blatantly lying. Even if she had done the same thing…

"Yes. Then I have to go away again right after."

So, he would be gone for New Year's. Guess that made it easier to decide on her plans. Though she would have preferred to ring in the New Year with him, she understood if he actually had to go on a work trip.

Unless he was lying about that, too…

Slippery slope.

"I'm sorry. I really can't talk right now." He sounded frustrated and impatient to be off the phone. "Stop trying to guilt-trip me!" he shouted.

Bryna peeked around the corner and saw him run an irritated hand back through his hair. His face was contorted into a scowl that she had never seen him use around her before. She swallowed hard at the realization of who this might actually be.

"I'm getting off the phone now. Have a merry Christmas." He tossed the phone onto the granite counter, rested his palms on the edge, and hung his head forward.

She knew she should give him a minute, but she wanted him to know she had heard at least part of his conversation. *No reason to hold that back.*

"So, that was your wife, huh?" Bryna asked, stepping into the kitchen.

Jude jumped and then turned to face her. "Bri."

"I thought you were separated."

"I thought you were asleep."

"I woke up," she said with a shrug.

"How much of that did you hear?" he asked.

She wasn't sure exactly what he was thinking. He wasn't one to wear his emotions on his sleeve unless he wanted her to see them. *Did he not want me to know he was talking to his wife?*

"Enough to realize that someone calling you on Christmas morning and asking about your New Year's plans is probably someone important. Oh, and she upset you. I've never seen you upset," she told him point-blank.

"Was," he corrected. "She *was* someone important, and we *are* separated. That's why I'm here with you." He walked across the tile floor and wrapped his arms around her. "This is the only place I want to be. She doesn't matter to me."

If Bryna were a typical girl, she might have just let the subject drop. After all, it was Christmas, she was in St. Barts on vacation, and the man she was falling for had just said that there was nowhere else he'd rather be.

Except she wasn't typical.

"So…are you guys getting a divorce then?"

Jude took a step back and sighed. "Merry Christmas to you, too."

"Oh. Merry Christmas," she said. "In California, I know you have to be separated for at least six months before a divorce is finalized."

"Can we not talk about this?" he asked. He looked weary of the topic of discussion.

"Ever?"

He grabbed her by the back of her thighs, hoisted her legs around his waist, and then carried her to the island in the middle of the kitchen. "Not while you're here in nothing but skimpy lingerie."

His mouth landed hot on her neck, and he kissed his way up to her earlobe. Her brain started going fuzzy again. Fuck, she wanted to just forget all the questions she had been asking. This felt so fucking good.

She pulled back and gave him a stern look. "Are you trying to distract me?"

"I'm going to make you come. Are you objecting?"

Well, when he puts it that way… "No."

His fingers dug into her thighs as their lips came together once more. He was intoxicating. Their chemistry was electric. Every touch threatened to push her over the edge and liquidate her very existence. She was already lost in the moment, in his tender caresses, and in thrall to his mesmerizing ways.

Jude pushed her back until she was lying flat on the island and then slid her down until her ass was almost hanging off the edge. He dragged her underwear to the ground, and his followed. His fingers gently probed her pussy, swirling around her opening until it was slick, and then he rubbed his thumb along her clit. Her body heated as he warmed her up to his touch.

If Jude was purposely diverting her, this was clearly the best kind of distraction.

"Tell me you want me," he said. He teasingly slid his dick along her opening, not going in but making her want him more and more.

"Fuck, Jude. I want you. Just fuck me."

"Maybe if you ask nicely."

He pressed the tip against her, and she gave up the illusion of control. She tilted her head back, closed her eyes, and arched toward him.

"Please," she groaned. "Please take me. I'm yours."

"Yes"—he shoved inside her pussy—"you are."

After his declaration, their bodies smacked together in time. It was feral and possessive, a joining of two beings out of a basic primal craving. No thoughts crossed their minds of what awaited them once they rejoined reality. There was nothing else but the thrill of taking what they wanted, living without guilt for their choices and enjoying every fucking minute of it.

BRYNA SILENCED HER PHONE for the second time that morning. Celia kept calling her, and Bryna did not want to talk to her. *If my own father hadn't called, why would my stepmother think that I would want to talk to her?*

She had thought about calling her father in New Zealand, but he was the parent. *Shouldn't he care enough to call or at least text?* He was a modern man. He knew how to use a smartphone, and he had an unlimited international package plan, so he could use his phone anywhere at anytime. Apparently, that time didn't include calling his daughter on Christmas.

She didn't want to let that bother her. Not today while she was spending the wonderful day with someone who actually cared for her.

Her eyes cut across the pool to where Jude was swimming laps. His shoulders and back were ripped. While he wasn't bulky, he had great definition. She couldn't tear her eyes away. They'd had sex before breakfast, but when he was half naked in front of her, it wasn't fair how much she wanted him. He made her insatiable.

Her phone started buzzing again, and she grumbled under her breath. *How distracting!*

She went to silence the ringer when she noticed that Gates was calling, not her stepmother. She rolled her eyes but answered anyway.

"Merry Christmas," she said faux-cheerfully.

"Bri, where the fuck are you?" Gates asked.

She froze. Gates sounded freaked out.

"Why? What's wrong?"

"I just got a call from Celia. You haven't answered your phone all morning, so she called your mother."

"She *what?*" Bryna shrieked, sitting up in her lounge chair.

Jude's head popped up out of the water at the commotion. He wore a concerned look on his face. "Everything all right?"

She covered the phone to hopefully muffle any noise and nodded at Jude. She hoped she didn't look as terrified as Gates had sounded. Because this was fucking terrible. "Yeah. Just a call from home," she told him, trying to hold on to a smile.

"All right," he said. His brows furrowed, but he went back to swimming. At least there was one benefit of his sneaky conversation this morning. No questions.

"Who are you with?" Gates demanded.

"It doesn't matter. I cannot believe Celia had the audacity to call my mother. What a bitch! How dare she question me like that and reach out to my mother just because I didn't answer some stupid phone call.

You would think she suspected me of doing something wrong!"

"Well…aren't you?" he asked.

"Whatever," she said. "Wait, how do you know all of this?"

"Because when Celia realized that you weren't, in fact, spending Christmas break with your mom, she went off the deep end trying to find out where you *actually* were and called me."

Bryna's stomach dipped. This wasn't good. This wasn't good at all. "Why would she call you?"

"I don't know, Bri," he said exasperated. "Maybe because I'm the only friend you have."

Bryna rolled her eyes again. "Please."

"And I'm your ex, so it would be reasonable to assume that we had snuck away together, which is what I told Celia when she called."

"You covered for me?" She breathed out a sigh of relief. *Thank God!*

"What the fuck was I supposed to say?" He groaned and muttered curses under his breath. "Fuck, Bri. I don't want to be in the middle of this shit. You're obviously with some other fucking guy somewhere, and here I am, still covering for you with your family."

"Cut the shit. You didn't have to cover for me. I know you too well. You did it because you want something. What is it?" she asked. She was grateful that Gates had told Celia they were together, but he hadn't done it out of his own good grace. He was a schemer much like she was, and if he had done something generous, it was because he wanted something from her for the favor.

Gates exhaled softly into the phone. "I did have to cover for you. While you might choose to believe you have other friends, I know that you're the closest thing to a real friend I have. Even if you are a total psycho sometimes, Bri."

"How charming."

"Come with me for New Year's."

"There it is," she muttered. Of course. She should have known. "I knew you wanted something out of this."

"You already knew I wanted you to come with me."

"You have to fucking promise not to tell anyone about me being gone," she insisted.

"It's not an I'll-fucking-tell-if-you-don't kind of thing," Gates cried. "I told Celia you were with me, and you will be until you get back. I'm a man of my word."

"Good, because if that isn't the case, be sure to remember that I know about you and Chloe."

"Jesus, Bri!" he griped. "You don't have to blackmail me to keep a secret."

"Just making sure."

She couldn't let anyone find out about her being away with Jude. Things were finally starting to get on the right track, and she couldn't risk anything going wrong. As much as she wanted to trust Gates, it was always easier to have dirt on the other person to ensure that they kept their mouth shut.

"Well, are you going to come with me?" Gates asked.

She glanced back down at Jude slicing through the water. He had said that he would be out of town for business on New Year's. It wouldn't hurt anything to go with Gates. "Fine. I'll go but *just* as friends."

"Sweet," he said, excitement in his voice. "Have fun on your trip."

"Yeah, thanks. Tell Chloe I said hi," she said, laughing lightly at the end.

"Don't be a bitch, Bri."

"All I know how to be."

Sometime later, Jude hoisted himself out of the pool. Water dripped down his body, and his soaked shorts clung to his legs. Bryna couldn't tear her eyes away. He lazily smiled at her as if he didn't already know that she was staring at him with desperate need.

"So," he said, taking a seat on her lounger. He planted a kiss on her lips, and water trickled down her white bathing suit.

"So," she muttered. She ran her fingers up into his dark wet hair and tugged him back down for another kiss.

"I might have planned something for you today."

She arched an eyebrow. "You took me on a private plane to Saint Barts. I don't think you need to plan anything else!"

"But I like to," he said, looking meaningfully into her eyes. "You appreciate it."

"I do." Their fingers interlocked, and she leaned into him. "I love this."

He kissed the top of her head. She didn't need any other plans if they could do this all day. Being here with him was enough.

But he did have plans, and she wasn't going to keep him from them if he had made them for her.

"So, what are we doing?" she asked.

"*You* are going to the spa. I have a car waiting to take you into town, and when you come back, put on something nice."

"And what will you be doing?"

"That is a surprise," he said with a devious smile. "You'll find out when you get back."

More surprises? *This man is full of them.* "A spa day does sound pretty amazing."

"I thought you might think so. The car will be here shortly." He stood up and helped her to her feet. "I can't wait to see you when you get back."

He kissed her until they were both breathless, and she considered skipping the spa to stay in the bedroom. But he reluctantly pulled away with a chuckle and scooted her toward the house. She wistfully looked back at him, and then she scurried inside to change before meeting the car waiting for her downstairs.

Bryna spent the entire afternoon at the spa. The resort spa took comfort to a new level. They needed this kind of heaven in Los Angeles. By the time she left the place, she felt more relaxed than she had in years.

When she returned, a butler directed her up the back stairs to the bedroom. The spa had blown out her hair and done her makeup. She opened up the closet and pulled out a shimmery gold dress. It was the fanciest piece she had brought with her, and she hadn't ever thought that she would have a place to wear it on this trip, but she had wanted to be prepared for anything.

The form-fitting material clung to her body like it had been made specifically for her. It dropped to her knees and had a tiny button at the back of her neck with a long open slit down the middle of her back. She paired it with black Jimmy Choos and clasped the gold buckles around her ankles.

After assessing herself in the mirror, she grabbed the Christmas present she had gotten for Jude from her suitcase before walking out of the bedroom and into the living room. Her eyes nearly bugged out when she saw everything he had done.

The room was completely decked out in Christmas decorations. A tree—a *real* freaking Christmas tree—sat in one corner with red ornaments and a star on top. She had no fucking clue where he had gotten that on an island in the middle of the Caribbean. Red and green pillows were on the furniture, decorated wreaths were hooked to the windows, stockings hung from the built-in bookshelves, and candles burned everywhere. The television was even set to appear as if an open fire was blazing in the fireplace.

Jude was standing in the middle of the room in a tuxedo, drinking a glass of scotch. He smiled at the shocked look on her face. "Merry Christmas, beautiful."

"What *is* all of this?"

"Well, I didn't exactly bring you somewhere that is very festive. Since we didn't end up in New York City or Paris where we could do Christmas activities, I thought that maybe I could bring Christmas to you."

"It's…amazing," she breathed. Truly, she was mesmerized.

"I'm glad you like it. Christmas has always been my favorite holiday. I used to go to Tahoe and go skiing with my parents when I was younger. But once I grew up, I usually worked too much around the holidays to really enjoy myself. So, thank you. I'm enjoying Christmas this year because of you," he said, pulling her into his arms.

"You did all the work."

"But you made it worthwhile."

She stared up at him, speechless. *How did I get so lucky on that night at Allure to go home with this incredible man?* She'd had no idea what she was getting into, and she didn't regret a minute of it. He was handsome and charming. He took care of her, appreciated her, enjoyed her company. In fact, her company was enough for him, which was something she had never experienced before.

"Before we go into the dining room to eat dinner, I do have a Christmas present for you," he told her.

"Me first," she said, remembering that she was holding his present in her hands.

He laughed and took the small box from her. "You didn't have to get me anything."

"I wanted to."

After setting his scotch down on the glass coffee table, he pulled back the gold-and-silver wrapping paper and opened the box to reveal a silver Rolex with a black face.

The week before, she had been frustrated while looking for a present for him. She had wanted to get something extravagant, something to match the gifts he had gotten her. But she wouldn't have access to her trust fund until July, and she hadn't wanted to draw attention to her credit card with an obscene charge. She could chalk up a Rolex as a gift for Gates.

He slipped the watch out of the box and slid it on to his wrist. Then, he wrapped his other arm around her waist and crushed his mouth down on hers. She smiled against his lips.

"You're amazing. Thank you."

"I'm glad you like it."

She had been unreasonably afraid that he would toss the watch aside because it wasn't up to his standards. She had known the idea was irrational, but it had still eaten away at her. She had never felt like this before, and she wasn't sure what to make of it, except that she liked him enough to care about his opinion.

"My turn."

He reluctantly released her before picking up a slender red-wrapped box. She slowly tore away the paper to reveal a navy-blue box with *HW* printed in gold on the top.

She swallowed and anxiously looked up at him. "Harry Winston?"

He took the box from her hand and pried it open for her to see the contents. Inside was a cursive *B* gold pendant inlaid with a series of exquisite diamonds on a slender gold chain.

"Oh my God," she whispered.

Jude removed the necklace from the box, and when she reached up to pull her hair off her back, he secured it at the nape of her neck. It rested against her skin just below her collarbone.

He pressed his lips to her shoulder. "There. It's perfect."

"You're   perfect,"   she   murmured   before kissing him.

Dinner could wait.

TWENTY-ONE

"Bryna! How was your trip with Gates?" Celia asked as soon as Bryna stepped through the door.

"Great," she said hollowly.

She dropped her Louis Vuitton luggage in the foyer.

The plane had landed only an hour ago, and already, she was feeling jet-lagged. The remainder of the trip had been a dream come true. She and Jude had spent seven full days together, and in that time, she had found that she liked him even more. She liked him so much, in fact, she felt his absence like a weight in the pit of her stomach. Leaving had been a true test of control. She was already desperate to return to her slice of paradise.

She just wanted to drive back to his apartment and stay there for as long as she could.

Unfortunately, Jude would be leaving the next morning on business, so that wasn't a possibility. Somehow, between the time she had left Jude's place for home to when she would leave with Gates to go to the Chateau Marmont New Year's party, she would have to come down from the high she had been riding on cloud nine.

"I really wish you had told me that you were going to spend time with Gates," Celia crooned. "I would have preferred you were with family for the holidays, of course, but I understand that you wanted to spend time with your boyfriend."

"That's great, Celia," Bryna said dryly.

"So, what did you do? Did you two have a good time? I'm sure you're mother missed your terribly. I know we did here, and your father as well."

Bryna sighed dramatically. Coming down from this high was going to be easier than she had thought. "Can we talk about this later? I'm really tired. I didn't get much sleep while I was gone." She let the implication of her words sink in.

"Oh, uh…sure. I'm glad you're home," Celia said.

"Yeah." That made one of them.

Bryna ascended the steps and crashed into her bedroom.

She slept for a couple of uninterrupted hours and only got up because she was starving. When she came downstairs to scrounge up something for dinner, Pace was in the kitchen. It was hard to believe that she had been eating incredible meals with Jude in St. Barts just this past week.

"You look tan," Pace muttered before biting into a peanut butter sandwich.

Don't engage. Retract claws. "Yep."

She reached into the fridge, and she pulled out an apple and a bottle of Pellegrino. She wasn't going to waste any more time in the kitchen if Pace intended to stick around. Eating out sounded like a better option.

"You weren't really with Gates, were you?"

She bit into her apple and didn't respond. She didn't want to have this conversation. She tried to imagine herself back in the villa—lounging beside the pool, Jude swimming, the feel of his body pressing against hers as he took her in the cabana. Soon, that would be her life, and she wouldn't have to deal with Pace anymore. She would get into LV State and spend her weekends with Jude in Los Angeles.

Her fantasies were distracting her enough that she missed whatever Pace had said.

"I don't know what you just said, but I really don't care." She started toward the exit.

"I saw Gates on the *Today* show for *Broken Road*. That show is in New York City."

"Really?" she said. Her eyes went wide, and her mouth dropped open in mock shock. "Groundbreaking. Who knew that the *Today* show was in New York?"

"It was snowing."

"And?" she snapped. *God, can't he just spit out what he's trying to say?*

He eyed her curiously. He clearly thought he had her all figured out. "How did you come back from Christmas in New York with a tan?"

Bryna shrugged, nonplussed. "Ever heard of a tanning bed?"

"I have. I don't think you use them."

147

His eyes traveled down her body, and she shuddered at the attention. He made her feel so disgusting.

She snapped her fingers at him. "Would you cut that shit out?"

Obviously realizing he wasn't getting anywhere with that line of reasoning, he changed tactics. "Where did you get that necklace?"

Her hand immediately reached for the diamond necklace at her throat. A smile spread on her face at the thought of Jude's Christmas present. "Gates got it for me," she lied.

"Gates has never gotten you a present before and certainly not anything with diamonds in it," he said suspiciously.

"Whatever, Pace. Just because you're jealous doesn't mean you have to be a dick and call everything into question," she snapped at him.

"Is that what you think?" he asked, moving forward until he was standing in front of her. "That I'm jealous of your boy toy? I'm jealous of your perfect life?"

She glared up at him. "What else could explain the slimy way you look at me? The way you try to tear apart my life? You're jealous because you will never be anything but Valley trash. You're an imposter in my world. You don't have the money that you flaunt, and you'll *never* have me."

"The fact that you think I want you, Bri, just shows how much of a conceited bitch you really are. You and your world disgust me more than you could ever know. But if you think I'm flaunting now, then just wait." He smirked down at her. "I finally get it now. Game on." He walked through the door and then thought better of it. "Have a good New Year's. I know I will."

Then, he was gone. She glowered after his back and mulled over what he had said. Had he not even been part of the game? Why else had he told her coach that she had skipped practice to go out? He knew what he was trying to do. She wouldn't let him sabotage her life. There was no way he could compete with her schemes.

Anyway, the fact that he could look at her with a straight face and say he didn't want her or any part of her world was laughable. He stalked her like a predator after his prey. He played quarterback at Harmony. He wore two-thousand-dollar suit jackets. He clearly had a warped sense of vanity.

But if he was going to finally play her game, then she would be ready to take him down when the time came.

TWENTY-TWO

BRYNA STEPPED OUT of Gates's limo and onto the red carpet leading into the Chateau Marmont in West Hollywood. She wore an Oscar de la Renta black-and-white dress and Chanel pearl heels with black tips.

Photographers lined the event, frequently stopping Gates for pictures, as reporters asked him questions. Once they reached the end of the line, he tightly wrapped an arm around her waist and pulled her away from the cameras. "You ready for this?"

"Of course. It's going to be fun."

"Thanks for coming with me."

"Don't thank me yet," she said with a wink.

His laugh was one of complete ease, as if he didn't have a care in the world. "I've missed your crazy ass."

"You just missed me keeping *your* crazy ass in line. Everyone else feeds into your impulsiveness."

He gave her an are-you-fucking-kidding-me look. "*My* impulsiveness? Weren't you away at Christmas with some other guy? Not sure how much more impulsive you can get."

"If this is you fishing again, it's really not going to work," Bryna told him.

"So, is it the same guy?"

"We're not talking about this tonight. I'm here to get drunk with my friend and ring in the New Year. If you're not providing that, maybe I'll make new friends."

He tugged her closer. "Babe, making friends isn't your strong suit."

"Whatever. Let's just go get drinks."

Gates took her hand and walked her through the crowd inside the connected darkened ballrooms. There were dozens of A-list celebrities at this event. Even though she was used to seeing stars who her father had worked with, the sheer quantity was enough to make her head turn.

Then, she saw someone that really did make her head turn.

She caught a glimpse of the back of his suit—a black Hugo Boss, if she had to guess, tailored to fit. It was the same dark brown hair she had run her fingers through this week. She craned her neck to see if she could see his face or profile, but Gates was moving her away from the man, and she never got a good look.

Her mind whirred to life. *Was that Jude? Fuck!*

He wasn't supposed to be here. He'd said that he was going to be out of town on business. *But didn't I hear him say the exact same thing to his wife over Christmas?*

She wanted to march back over there and see if it was him, but she didn't want Gates to know she was doing it. Not to mention, if it really *was* Jude, she didn't want him to see her with Gates. Even though she and Gates were just friends, Jude wouldn't want to see her with another guy. And if he recognized Gates, then he might be able to piece together who *she* was...and how old she was. It was all one big headache.

She glanced over her shoulder and searched the crowd for the man. It couldn't have been Jude. *How many men in incredible suits with dark hair are here?* She had Jude on the brain. After all, she was missing him tonight. She had been missing him since she kissed him good-bye and left his apartment.

It was probably a trick of her imagination. She wanted him here with her, so she had conjured him up out of thin air.

But still, she kept looking for him, even when a few hours had passed, and she realized that her hope was futile. Hope was just a dull ache in her chest from missing him.

Bryna and Gates danced the night away, talking and laughing like old times. It felt nice to unwind with him. She had been spending all her free time with Jude, and she hadn't even realized that she missed hanging out with Gates until now.

"I'm having such a good time," she said as they moved off the dance floor and into a corner of the ballroom.

The clock was counting down to midnight, and everyone was cheering around them.

"Me, too. Do you remember last year, we were doing this at a Harmony party? Now, we're at Chateau Marmont."

Bryna tossed her head back and laughed at the thought. She was giddy from the alcohol, and her head felt heavy. But the thought of being at a Harmony party only a year ago was somehow hysterical.

She stumbled forward, catching herself on Gates's suit. When she righted herself, she rested her hand on his chest. He grabbed her arm and steadied her. Suddenly, she was lost in a sea of blue as he stared at her in a way she'd never seen before.

Then the crowd cheered for the New Year, and Gates was kissing her. His mouth was hot and familiar against hers. His fingers clung to the material of her dress and pressed herself against him. It only lasted a second before she ripped herself free of him and smacked him across the face.

"You said we were just friends!" she cried.

She stormed away from him. She couldn't believe this. It was such a bad idea for her to be here with him. She didn't know why she thought they could be friends. They obviously couldn't. It was time to get out of here.

Gates ran after her. "Bri," he called.

He grabbed her arm and pulled her out of the ballroom and into a private sitting room. She wrenched her arm away from him.

"Bri, I know you said we were just friends," he pleaded.

"Yet you're not sorry about kissing me," she said accusingly.

"No, I'm not." He gestured for her to take a seat, and he sat next to her.

"You promised, Gates."

"I promised that I wouldn't fucking tell anyone that you were with some stranger over Christmas instead of with me," he cried. "I never promised that I would come here as friends. That was all you."

"Well, I wasn't lying to you! We're not together anymore. You can't go around kissing me."

"Who is this guy?" he demanded. He searched her eyes as if they told the source of his distress. "Why is the whole thing such a secret?"

"Because he is! What does it matter, Gates? I'm with him and not you."

"So where is he then? Not here with you in public," he said cruelly. "Just hidden away so no one can see you with him."

"He has a business trip for your information, and anyway I don't need to explain myself to you," she said, standing in a hurry. "I said we were just friends and you took advantage of that."

"*I* took advantage of you? Please! This guy is taking advantage of you. Why are you even with him?"

"Because unlike you, he understands me!"

Gates snorted, standing to face her. "You barely know him. How could he understand you? I don't even completely get your crazy."

"Exactly. He gets me and he cares about me and he takes care of me."

"He takes care of you?" Gates asked in confusion. "Your father is a fucking director, Bri. No one needs to take care of you."

"Well, maybe I like that he does *anyway*."

"Is that what this necklace is?" he asked, flicking the B around her neck.

"Christ, don't touch it! It's Harry Winston."

Gates's eyes turned round as saucers. "The guy is buying you Harry Winston? What does he do?"

Bryna glanced away from him. She didn't know the answer to that question. She had some ludicrous theories. The way Jude talked about his job made it seem like he was a pimp or a drug dealer or a male escort. But there was no way. She was sure that Jude was just in investments or something.

"What does it matter?" she asked.

"That's a Bryna sidestep. Queen bee doesn't know the answer."

"I do," she lied.

He stared her straight in the eyes and shook his head. "What do you even know about this guy? He could be anyone."

"Don't worry about me. I can take care of myself."

"Hey," he said. "I know I kissed you, but I do want to be here for you as a friend. I don't want to see you get hurt. So...be careful."

She smiled at Gates with a confidence she didn't feel. "I don't need to be. I know exactly what I'm doing." When she turned to leave, she wondered if she knew what she was doing at all.

Gates caught up with her again and gave her an apologetic look. "I'm really sorry. I don't want you to be mad at me. I only ask because I care about you."

Bryna looked off into the distance. "I know you do, but you have to trust me when I say we're just friends."

"I get it. Can I still take you home?"

After a minute, she nodded. "Yeah."

They walked out of the hotel together and into his limo. They were silent on the ride home. Their friendship was intact, and she felt better knowing that he wasn't going to try anything. It was also kind of nice that someone knew about Jude even if Gates didn't have any of the details. It was like a weight off of her chest.

When they were more than halfway to her house, her phone buzzed in her clutch. She peeked at the name, and her heart skipped. "Gates, you don't mind if I take this call, do you?"

"Is it him?"

She couldn't keep from smiling at the thought of Jude calling her, so she just nodded.

"Go for it." Gates turned toward the window to give her a semblance of privacy.

She answered the phone. "Hey! Happy New Year!"

"Happy New Year," Jude said.

The phone was scratchy, as if there was loud music somewhere in the background.

"Where are you? I can barely hear you."

"Oh, sorry," he said. After a couple of seconds, the music died down to a soft buzz. "Didn't realize it was that loud. I'm at a party for work."

"I didn't know that's what you meant by work." She tried not to sound like she was pouting, but wasn't sure how well she pulled it off.

"I'm sure it's not half as much fun as what you're doing."

She glanced out the window, lamenting a New Year's without him. "I mostly miss you."

"I miss you, too. I think I'm seeing things because I swore, I saw a girl who looked just like you."

Bryna laughed. "Same thing happened to me. But you're not even in L.A., so it must have been someone else."

"Must have been," he agreed. "Where did you end up tonight anyway?"

"Oh, Chateau Marmont."

There was a pause before he asked, "By yourself?"

"No. I was with a friend of mine."

"A guy friend?"

"Yeah, but you have nothing to worry about. We're just friends. Where did you fly out to anyway? You're full of questions. I think you can answer one yourself."

There was silence on the other end for long enough that she shifted awkwardly in her seat.

"Are you still there?" she asked.

"I didn't go out of town."

"You didn't?" she asked, confused. "Why did you tell me that you did?"

"I was at Chateau Marmont tonight. I didn't know you'd be there, but I saw you kiss someone else, Bri."

Her stomach dropped, and she gripped the seat. "No. You have it all wrong. I wasn't…it wasn't what it looked like."

"We weren't playing a game. I wasn't coming to snatch you away. You were just with him," he accused

"Jude, I swear, that is not what happened. He's a friend. It meant *nothing* to me."

Gates snapped his head in her direction, and she waved him away.

This could not be happening. She couldn't be dealing with this. *Why the fuck is Jude in town? And why was he at the same hotel as me?* He was supposed to be somewhere at work where it wouldn't matter that she was out with a friend. And he had seen Gates kiss her but obviously not the slap afterward.

Fuck!

She was shaking, literally trembling in her seat.

"I have to get back to the party. Let's talk about this tomorrow."

"Jude," she whispered.

"Good night, Bri."

The line went dead, and she dropped her phone into her lap in disbelief.

"Are you okay?" Gates asked, reaching for her.

She swallowed hard and tried to hold in her pain. She wouldn't unravel. She was strong, confident, and independent. She didn't need a guy. She didn't need…

Tears silently pooled in her eyes, and she turned into Gates's shoulder.

He held her against him. "Tell me what happened."

"He saw you kiss me."

"He was there?" Gates asked in surprise.

"I didn't know he'd be there."

"So…did you guys break up?" He sounded cautious and uncertain.

He wasn't used to comforting her. She didn't normally need comforting. This was all new territory for her.

"He said he wants to talk tomorrow."

"I'm sorry, Bri. I never would have done that if I'd known. I would never want to upset you."

She put her head in her hands and leaned forward. "What am I going to do?"

"Blame it on me. He's just angry right now. It'll be okay."

"I hope you're right."

TWENTY-THREE

JUDE DIDN'T CALL THE NEXT DAY.

Or the day after that.

On the third day, Bryna couldn't hold it in any more, and she dialed his phone number. It rang forever before clicking over to voice mail. She tried one more time. When it went to voice mail again, she left a quick message asking him to call her. She couldn't bring herself to call again. She wasn't going to act fucking desperate.

Clearly, it didn't matter that he had said they would talk on New Year's Day. He had lied about leaving Los Angeles. Why wouldn't he lie about him calling too?

She still couldn't believe that he had actually been at Chateau Marmont on New Year's. She had been safe and secure in the knowledge that things with

Gates were platonic and that nothing could go wrong. Then, she had been smacked in the face with *this*.

Her feelings for Jude were the same as when they had spent a week together in St. Barts. She didn't know how he could feel differently in such a short period of time. Nor did she know how he could go this long without talking to her and getting clarification on what had really transpired. If she had seen him with someone else, she would have wanted a goddamn explanation.

Bryna tried to go about her normal life, but everything felt surreal with school starting again. It was as if the entire Christmas break had been a dream…and then a nightmare.

She was glad she had so much to occupy her time and keep her mind off of what had happened.

Competition season was coming up for cheer, so they were doubling practices. And Felicity wanted to start weekly meetings to discuss the charity benefit. Bryna selected three assistants—Avery, Tara, and Jemma—to ease the load. Though Avery and Tara were being weird and distant. Bryna didn't know what that was about, but she couldn't even bother with it.

College applications had to be turned in by this weekend, and she was trying to focus on planning out her campus visit schedule. She had already turned in her LV State application, but she still had to finish up UCLA, Stanford, Berkeley, and NYU. She kept trying to tell herself that there were more important things to do than stress about Jude, her friends, and cheer.

Later that week, after practice, she drove home from school with her mind full of everything she needed to accomplish. She parked her car in the garage and took the stairs two at a time. Just as she entered her bedroom, she saw Pace peek out from his room.

"Leave me alone," she called before slamming the door.

As she expected, two seconds later, he was opening the door.

She plopped down at her desk, turning her back to him. "I said, leave me alone."

"Have a good practice?"

"I don't want to make small talk with you. I want you to get out of my room," she commanded. Pace was the last person she wanted to deal with when her temper was on a short fuse.

Pace continued to ignore her and lounged on her bed. "You've been a mega bitch lately, more so than normal. Trouble in paradise?"

Bryna closed her eyes and counted to five before responding, "No. I'm just busy."

"Well," he said, smiling mischievously, "I came by to tell you something."

"What?" she snapped.

"The president's assistant at LV State called twice. She was asking for you, about some campus recruitment weekend. I told them you were considering other options and to try back another time."

"What?" she asked, standing abruptly.

"Have a nice afternoon."

He started to stride out of the room with confidence when she burst out laughing.

He turned and glared at her. "What's so funny?"

"Is this your idea of sabotage?" She shook her head. "You're going to have to do better than that. Don't you know that my father is a fucking booster at

LV State? If they hear that I'm considering other schools, they'll be clamoring for me to come visit. Don't want their money to dry up."

Pace pursed his lips as he seemed to realize his mistake. He looked pissed that whatever he had planned wasn't going to work. It was cute that he had thought he could destroy her chance at LV State, but really, that wasn't happening.

"So, thanks for that." She smirked and waggled her fingers at him. "You can go now."

He seemed to consider her for a moment. His eyes bore into hers. "Well, I was going to wait for your friends to tell you, but I slept with Avery and Tara over New Year's."

Bryna's mouth dropped open before she could stop herself. She quickly covered her look of disbelief. "They wouldn't touch you."

The laughter in his eyes made her reconsider. Her friends were kind of dumb, but surely, they had known what this would mean for them. They both knew what she thought about Pace and how it had looked for her to have him at Harmony. She didn't exactly confide in them, but they still *knew*. Fuck, everyone did.

"You wouldn't," he said. "But they did. Both of them. At the same time."

Just the thought of that made her want to lose her lunch.

Bryna gagged.

"Tara did some of that. Avery doesn't have a gag reflex though. It's amazing."

"I don't believe you. Just get out of my room. Now."

She jumped out of her desk chair, charged at him, and shoved against him, trying to throw him out of her room, but he was solid. He barely moved more than a few inches.

"I will beat you at your own game, Bri. This is only the beginning."

He backed out of her room, and she slammed the door again.

Her heart was racing. *Could it be true that Avery and Tara slept with my fucking stepbrother? Ugh!* It was too disgusting to think about. Maybe Pace was only planting a seed in her mind to try to freak her out, or maybe they had really gone through with it. Either way, she had to know the truth.

She jotted out a text to her friends to meet her at a coffee spot off Rodeo under the pretenses of finding a dress for the charity benefit, and then she dashed out of her house.

Fifteen minutes later, she was seated at her favorite outdoor table with a skinny mocha macchiato in front of her.

Avery and Tara showed up a few minutes later.

Avery smiled brightly and tossed her hair. "Hey, B. No Jemma?"

"I thought we could look for dresses without her."

"Thank God," Tara said, collapsing into a chair.

"Mmm," Bryna murmured. She took a sip of her drink.

If what Pace had told her were true, Jemma would be the least of their concerns.

"So," Avery said once they had gotten their drinks, "where do you want to go first?"

Bryna folded her hands in her lap and stared at her two friends. "Probably Barneys." She took another sip of her drink and smiled. "It's so nice to be here with you guys. We haven't spent any time together outside of practice since we went to X. How was your break?"

Tara shifted and glanced at Avery. "Mine was good."

"Mine, too," Avery agreed.

"Good. The highlight for me was going to Chateau Marmont with Gates for New Year's." Of course, it had really been St. Barts with Jude, but the realities of her break had nothing to do with the true purpose of this conversation. "Where were you guys for New Year's? I haven't heard you talk about it."

"Uh…" they both mumbled.

They exchanged another glance.

"I was at the Harmony party," Tara said.

"Yeah…me, too."

Bryna nodded thoughtfully. "Gates tried to kiss me at midnight, and we got into a huge fight. Please tell me your night ended up better than that!"

"Mine was totally lame," Tara admitted.

"Mine, too," Avery parroted.

"Didn't kiss anyone at midnight?" Bryna asked.

Tara flushed and looked away. Avery tried to meet Bryna's eyes but didn't do a very good job of it. They both appeared anxious. Guilty.

Bryna held her silence. She watched them sit there and squirm. Soon enough, they would admit it. She couldn't believe this. The dirty whores had slept with her stepbrother. The way they were acting was proof enough that something had gone down.

After a full five minutes of dead silence, Tara broke. "I'm sorry, B."

"For?"

"Tara!" Avery snapped.

"She should know!"

"Know what?" Bryna prompted.

"I slept with Pace," Tara said. "So did Avery. Um...together on New Year's."

Bryna slowly stood from her seat and towered over her friends. "I already knew that," she said calmly.

They both looked like they might cry.

"Pace told me."

"What?" they both shrieked.

"That bastard," Avery cried.

"I can't believe him!" Tara said in horror.

"What I can't believe is that neither of you told me," Bryna admonished. "I had to hear it from him. And you know what? I actually defended you. Said that my friends would *never* touch him, and he proceeded to regale me with your lack of a gag reflex."

The girls paled further.

"Now, I'm wondering why I did that. You two know how disgusting Pace is, and how despicable it is to have to live with someone like that. The reason you didn't tell me was because you knew I would be pissed. Imagine how I feel now that I know you were hiding it."

She gave them a minute to consider what she had said.

"Bri, we didn't mean for it to happen," Avery insisted. "We were drunk, and he was there."

"We'd never do it again!" Tara cried.

Bryna shook her head. *Ridiculous and just plain insulting.* "You know how important this charity benefit is to me, and I need to make sure that it goes off without a hitch. So, you're both off the committee."

"What?" Avery shrieked.

Tara's jaw dropped to the floor. "You're serious?"

"I guess I'll go look for a dress by myself." She picked up her purse and smiled.

"You're really kicking us off the committee?" Avery demanded.

"Actions have consequences, girls. You just figured out what yours are," Bryna said.

She walked away from the coffee shop as she slid shades over her eyes and sighed. She couldn't let people think that they could get away with this kind of shit. She was still queen after all. She had to rule her queendom with an iron fist. What had happened was out of necessity.

She wished fixing the situation with Jude could be as easy as it had been with the girls.

TWENTY-FOUR

TWELVE DAYS.

It took Jude twelve days to call Bryna back.

She saw his name on her phone, and she wasn't sure which emotions she conjured first. Anger, joy, frustration, hope—they all hit her with an onslaught.

He's calling!

He's calling now after all this time? What took him so long?

She wouldn't know the answer to any of her questions if she didn't answer the phone. With a rush of courage, she swiped the touch screen to the side. "Hello?"

"Bri," he said in relief.

"Hi, Jude." Anger was winning out. *How dare he make me wait this long!*

"How are you?"

She remembered back to when she had first met him, and he had made her wait five weeks before he called. She had tried to be cool and collected, playing it off, but it had bothered her. And it bothered her more now.

"Frustrated and confused. I don't like to skirt around issues. We need to talk."

"You're right. I should have called you right away, like I said I would. I was pissed and irrational, but," he said softly, "Bri, I've missed you so much."

Her resolve weakened slightly at those words. *God, I've missed him.* Even if she was angry and uncertain about the state of their relationship, she had still wanted to rush over to him and make it all right. *How is he able to pull such emotions out of me?* "I missed you, too. But how could you make me wait like this? It's not like I was the only one in the wrong. You lied to me about where you were going to be. What were you even doing there?"

"I know. I had planned to be out of town for work, but I ended up staying in town instead."

"Why?" she asked. She had been thinking about this since that night. She couldn't figure out why he had skipped his work plans to go to the hotel for New Year's. There had to be a reason.

"I was still working. A lot of my clients were there that night."

"You keep saying that, but I don't know what it means. The more I think about it, the more my imagination runs away with me. What *do* you do?"

Jude sighed. "It's really not that crazy."

"Then, why do you have to hide it from me?"

"You act as if you don't have any secrets when I caught you kissing another man," he accused.

"I didn't kiss anyone. If you had let me explain instead of avoiding me, you would have known the truth."

"I saw what happened, Bri. I was standing right there."

"If you had been there the whole time, then you would have seen me slap him across the face and storm off. Because that's what I did!" she said, her voice rising.

"Really?" he asked. He sounded like he didn't believe her, but he wanted to. At least he was intrigued and listening to her side. She had wanted to say this for almost two weeks. Now the floodgates opened.

"Yes! I went with him as a friend, and then he got swept up in the moment at midnight. I chewed him out for trying anything because I'm dating you. I only want you." She felt her anger dwindling. It was replaced with sadness at the fact that any of this had to be said at all.

"Who was he?"

"Does it matter?" she asked. "Either you believe me when I say he is just a friend and I never intended for that to happen, or you don't."

The line was silent for a minute.

"I believe you. I simply wonder if you would have ever told me that he kissed you if I hadn't seen it for myself."

Would I have? Probably not. It hadn't meant anything to her, and he wouldn't have needed to know. She knew he would have been pissed. If she had been in his shoes and he had been with someone else on New Year's, she would have been pissed, too.

"I didn't think so," he said.

171

"What do you want me to say, Jude? I never would have hidden that I was with my friend on New Year's if we were able to be honest with each other. You could have told me that you were going to be at Chateau Marmont for work, and then we could have met up and had a proper New Year's kiss. Instead, we're stuck behind this veil of mystery. You won't trust me with your secrets, so how can I trust you with mine?" she asked hopelessly.

"You're right," he said softly. "I think it's time I tell you everything and let you decide what this is once you have all the facts."

"I'd like that."

In truth, it terrified her a bit. *What is he hiding that could make me change my mind about him? Will he change his mind about me? Guess I'll find out.*

"I can get away tonight," she told him.

He groaned. "Unfortunately, I'm not free until next weekend. This time, I actually am out of town. I'm in Chicago."

"Oh." *Great.* Just what she wanted to do, wait another week before they could get all of this out in the open. Not to mention—she missed him and wanted to be with him every second. His job was so inconvenient. Though it did have its advantages.

"How about next weekend?" he suggested.

She swallowed. "Sounds good."

It could all be over by next weekend.

TWENTY-FIVE

A WEEK LATER, Bryna walked into her last class. Her spot was open between Avery and Tara, but she hadn't been sitting in it since she had kicked them off the committee. She had replaced them with two other cheerleaders who had been ecstatic to see their stars rising.

She sat down in her new seat near the front of the room as her phone started buzzing noisily in her purse.

Fuck! Who the hell is calling me while I'm in school?

She checked the screen and smiled brightly.

"Miss Turner, please put your phone away," the teacher instructed. She looked annoyed that Bryna would even have it out, as if all the students didn't text through her class.

"It's my father calling from New Zealand. I have to take this," she said. She confidently strode from the room. "Dad!"

"Hey, sweetie!"

"I'm in the middle of school. Time difference is kind of killer."

"Sorry about that. I'll send an apology over to Harmony, but I had to speak with you. Did you talk with anyone from LV State?" he asked, his tone turning serious.

"No. Pace said someone called, but they didn't call back."

"That's funny because they called me, worried that my daughter wasn't interested in doing a campus visit. What is this I hear? You don't want to go to LV State? It's my alma mater, Bryna. Your mother's alma mater. It's where you belong," he insisted.

"I still want to go there. I didn't speak to anyone. It must have been Pace. He's been playing this silly game, but it's getting out of hand. He's trying to sabotage my college prospects," she said, playing on the sweet and innocent vibe.

"I'll deal with your stepbrother, Bryna. But you have to go to that college visit that they set up. They wanted me to be there this weekend, but just because I'm not in town doesn't mean you're exempt," he told her.

"This weekend?" she groaned. "I have plans this weekend."

"Break them. Your future is more important."

Fuck! She was supposed to have her big talk with Jude this weekend, and now, she had to call the whole thing off. And she couldn't even tell him where she was going to be, not without giving everything up

174

before they met in person. The whole thing was frustrating.

As soon as she left school, she called Jude to break the news to him. They would have to plan another day to talk about their problems. Hopefully they would be able to chat on Monday as long as he didn't leave again right away. He had a tendency to do that.

When she finally spoke to Jude, he seemed suspicious on the phone, but when she explained that it was an emergency, he backed down. After that call with her dad, there wasn't any way for her to get out of it, and she promised Jude she would make it up to him as soon as they could meet again.

She was packing for Las Vegas when Celia called up the stairs. "Bryna! Your boyfriend is here."

Bryna cringed. *Boyfriend.* She must be talking about Gates. It was all so fucking confusing. She couldn't tell Celia that she and Gates weren't dating without raising red flags about what had happened over Christmas, and she hated explaining anything to that dimwit. Hopefully, the air would be cleared up soon enough.

She stepped out into the hallway as Gates reached the top of the stairs. "Hey, B."

"Gates," she said with a nod. She gestured for him to follow her back into her room.

Once he was inside, he shut the door. His eyes surveyed the mess. "Well, I was going to see if you wanted to go out, but it looks like you're leaving."

"LV State invited me to a recruitment weekend."

"Vegas?" he asked, raising his eyebrows. "Can I come, too?"

"Don't you have shit to do with your movie?"

"Nah. I have some free time before I finish off the promotion. You still coming to the premiere with me?"

"Yeah. Yeah. That's fine," she said, distracted. "You can come to Vegas, too. Whatever."

"You okay? You seem out of it."

"Jude and I were supposed to have this big talk this weekend, but my dad found out about this weekend visit, so I have to go now. I'm so pissed, and I don't know how this talk is going to go at all."

She tossed an LV State T-shirt into her bag and then tried to force it closed. Gates pushed it down, zipping it for her.

"Try not to stress it, B. You clearly love the guy."

Bryna dropped the suitcase she had just picked up and stared up at him with terrified eyes. "What did you just say?"

"You love him, don't you?" Gates asked. The typical humor in his eyes was replaced with sadness.

"I...don't want to talk about this," she muttered.

Not with Gates.

Not with anyone.

Love. That was the biggest four-letter word out there.

Do I love Jude? Her throat closed up, and her palms started sweating. She felt sick.

No, she wasn't going to think about that.

"All right. Are you staying on campus, or should I get us a place at the Bellagio?" Gates asked, changing the subject.

"I'm supposed to stay on campus, but get us a room in case the place is shit," she suggested.

"Done."

Gates immediately got on the phone with his manager and asked him to book them a room on the Strip for the weekend. They stopped at Gates's place to pick up an overnight bag and then headed out.

They arrived on campus just off of the Vegas Strip late that night. After checking in at the visitor's center, she was given directions to the campus hotel. The room was nice enough that she decided to stay there.

Gates drove back to the Bellagio alone with big plans to go to the casino and stay up half the night playing blackjack.

She had a meeting the next day, so she got some much-needed sleep before heading to the president's building in the morning. His assistant directed her down the hall to a large conference room. She stepped inside a roomful of other students. She wondered what they were all being recruited for. *How many parents did the president personally contact to get them here?*

She saw President West speaking to a few students on the other side of the room. He smiled when he saw her, but she walked in the opposite direction. *Is he seeing me or dollar signs?*

She might have ended up here at her father's insistence, but she wanted to like LV State. It had always been her top choice. She had been on campus since she was a baby. She wanted to rule like she did now at Harmony. But with nearly fifty thousand students, would that be possible? The thought set her on edge. She wanted to find her people...now. She didn't want to wait for school to start to make friends and step into the limelight.

Bryna tried mingling with a few students and found out that many of them were there for a scholarship interview. They were finalists for a full-ride merit scholarship. She ended up sitting next to one of the girls during lunch with the president. The university had flown the girl in from some small town in Alabama, and she had a thick Southern drawl that made it difficult for Bryna to understand half of what she was saying. It was clear...these were not her people.

By the end of lunch, she was glad to skip the tour for her meeting with the head football coach, Coach Galloway. While he was a young coach, he had earned the spot at LV State two years ago after there was a scandal with the previous coach. Coach Galloway took the team to a national championship victory that year and wasn't planning to leave anytime soon. Her father had made it a point to become friends with him, so she was relatively well acquainted with him.

She walked into the athletic complex and straight to his office. She knocked twice.

"Come in."

She pushed open the door. "Coach Galloway, it's so great to see you again."

"Bryna, how are you?" He stood, shook her hand, and gave her a dimpled smile.

"Great. It's so good to be back on campus."

"Glad to hear that. Why don't you sit down?"

She took him up on his offer and sat in the chair opposite his desk.

"How is your father doing?"

Bryna held back her sigh. "He's filming on location in New Zealand, so he is incredibly busy."

"It was unfortunate that he couldn't attend the homecoming game this year. And we're missing him this weekend."

"So am I."

Everyone always asking about her dad. Between Gates and her dad, people were going to know who she was on campus all right. It made her second-guess the decision to bring Gates along…and second-guess this meeting as well.

"I'm sure he'll be around next year when I'm cheering on the sidelines."

Coach Galloway laughed jovially and nodded. "I'm sure he will."

A knock on the door sounded, and she turned around to see who was interrupting.

"Hey, Coach. You called for me?"

"I did. Bryna, let me introduce you to our student representative."

Bryna's smile brightened. "Eric Wilkins."

He turned at his name, and she drank him in. Six feet tall, dark brown hair, light honey–hazel eyes. He was still built as if he had never blown out his knee beyond recognition last year in the middle of his touchdown interception that won them the game during the national championship.

"I shouldn't be surprised you recognize him. Eric is training underneath me as a student coach," Coach Galloway told her. "Eric, this is Bryna Turner. Her father is Lawrence Turner, nineteen eighty-eight National Championship winner."

Eric nodded appreciatively and walked over to shake her hand. "I love his movies," he told her. "Clever work."

"Thanks," she murmured.

"If you don't mind, Eric, I'd love for you to show Bryna around. Her father is a *very* esteemed alumnus."

Bryna stared back at Coach Galloway in surprise. They really were bringing in the big guns if they were getting Eric Wilkins to show her around. She wondered how many millions of dollars her dad donated every year for her to be getting this kind of treatment.

"Of course, Coach."

"Well, I have some more business to attend to here. It was great seeing you again, Bryna. I'll probably make a surprise appearance at the Sunday send-off brunch, so we'll talk again there."

Bryna took that as her dismissal. She shook the coach's hand again and then left the office with Eric.

"So, what are your plans today?" Eric asked. "Campus tour? Sit through an information session on the school? Tour the dorms?"

She cringed. "No, thanks. I'd rather do what students actually do on campus."

He laughed. "Get drunk and play football?"

"Sounds like my scene," she told him truthfully. If she made friends now, then she would be one step closer to taking over the school.

"Then, we need to go to Posse."

TWENTY-SIX

BRYNA MET UP WITH GATES AND ERIC on campus later that evening to go to Posse. The guys seemed to size each other up when they were introduced. They were about the same height, but Eric had a bigger build. Gates had lost some of the insane definition he had needed while on set for *Broken Road.*

After a few seconds, they smiled and shook hands.

They walked off campus to the club Eric had recommended. Gates and Eric talked easily the whole way while Bryna was lost in thought.

If her father hadn't forced her to come to this recruitment weekend, she would be locked away in Jude's apartment, discussing everything they had been holding back. Instead, she was on campus, being escorted by two guys who would probably sleep with her with a snap of her fingers.

She wasn't looking forward to explaining all of that to Jude once they finally made their confessions. Then again, it was nothing compared to the fact that she was seventeen and still in high school.

"This is the place," Eric said.

Posse was a colossal building with a bright green neon sign on the front. Eric got them past the bouncer and inside. The interior was a giant open space with multiple bars and tiered balconies overlooking the dance floor. A DJ blasted hip-hop music. Outside, there was a pool with several swim-up bars. The room had an energy that she couldn't explain. It was hypnotic.

She and Gates followed Eric through the crowd to one of the bars. He shook hands with a bunch of huge football players, and then he introduced them. She got a couple of appreciative looks and just kept her smile on her face. This was what she wanted to be doing next year—cheering on the sidelines, hanging out with football players, and overall, being the most desired person at the school. She needed to push Jude out of her thoughts tonight and enjoy her time here.

"Drink?" Eric offered.

"Yeah," she said, leaning her chest against the bar. "What's good here?"

He smiled down at her and pressed himself into the space between her and the guy behind him. They were nearly touching.

"Everything."

She glanced away from him and back toward the bar. She knew he was only flirting with her because the coach had told him to accommodate her.

Couldn't lose any of their booster money. But still, he was good at it.

"I'd like a dirty martini," she finally told him.

"If you like martinis, I'd recommend the Peppermint Posse."

"I'm in."

Eric flagged the bartender, and she scooted out from the bar. If Jude weren't in her life, she would have been all over Eric. But not tonight. When the bartender appeared in front of him, Eric ordered her martini and himself a beer. Gates already had one in hand from another blonde bartender. She must have recognized him because her mouth was dropped open in surprise.

Her Peppermint Posse drink was not only delicious, but it was also potent. She could feel her buzz setting in quickly.

By the time their group walked outside, she lost count of how many martinis she had consumed. Eric was talking to a couple of football players nearby. They kept shooting glances in her direction. Gates was by her side but talking to another blonde. She kept looking at Bryna as if wondering her relationship to Gates and how soon she could get him away from Bryna.

Bryna ignored the girl and motioned for another martini from a passing waiter. The waiter brought her the drink, and she started downing it. *God, this stuff is amazing.*

"Gates," Bryna whispered, leaning into him.

"Bri, not right now." He moved closer to the other girl.

"I'm going to call Jude."

He furrowed his brows. "Not a good idea. You're drunk."

"I'm fine," she slurred.

Her eyes wandered back over to Eric. He met her gaze and smiled before continuing to talk to the other players.

"Oh, and, Gates?"

"Yeah, B?"

"Don't you think Eric is hot?"

Gates sighed and shook his head. He excused himself from the girl he was talking to and walked them a short distance away. "I don't think that's a good idea either. You're *really* drunk."

"Do you think *he* thinks I'm hot?" she asked. Her head felt beyond fuzzy. She could barely keep her eyes open. *What the fuck was in those drinks?*

"Every guy in this place thinks you're hot, Bri. Because you are. And if I didn't know you loved someone else back in Los Angeles, I would drag you out of this bar, back to our hotel room, and fuck you."

Bryna softly patted his cheek. "That sounds fun."

Gates closed his eyes and ran a hand back through his hair. "We should go. I should take you back to campus."

"But I'm having so much fun!"

He moved her to a lounge chair and sat her down. "I'm going to let Eric know we're leaving. Don't move your crazy ass out of this seat."

"Or you'll spank it?" she asked, giggling.

"Just don't move it, okay?"

As soon as he walked away, she pulled out her phone and dialed Jude's number.

He answered groggily, "Bri?"

"Jude! Oh my God, I miss you."

"Are you drunk?" he asked.

"No. Okay, maybe."

He sighed. "Where are you?"

"Las Vegas," she told him. "I fucking love this city."

"Are you safe? Is everything okay? Do I need to come out there and get you?" He was gradually growing more fearful.

"No, don't worry. I'm with Gates. He's taking care of me," she said completely nonchalant.

"Who the hell is Gates?" Jude asked. His voice shifted to something dark that she didn't recognize in her state.

"My ex-boyfriend, but don't worry. We're just friends now."

"You are in Las Vegas with your ex-boyfriend…instead of in Los Angeles with me?"

"Yeah. But I'm visiting LV State, and Eric Wilkins is here!"

"Bri, what the fuck is going on with you? You're with your ex and a college football player? Do you even know what those guys are like?"

"It's not like that," she insisted. "We're just having a good time."

"I know guys like him and their idea of a good time," he said menacingly.

Gates walked back over right then. "Bri, what the fuck are you doing? Get off the goddamn phone."

"Who is that?" Jude asked.

"That's Gates. Here, talk to him!" She handed the phone off to Gates and flopped back on the lounge chair.

Gates took the phone out of her hand and stared at it before answering, "Hey, man. I'm sure this sounds really bad, but I'm just taking your girl back to her room, so she can sleep."

After a few seconds, Gates responded again through gritted teeth, "Yeah. I understand you perfectly." He hung up the phone and tossed it back into Bryna's purse. "Let's go."

"Is Jude coming?"

"No," he said, putting his arm under her shoulders and helping her up.

"Can Eric come?"

"You're not his type."

"But why? I thought I was everyone's type." She squinted up at him, and then her eyes went wide. "Oh my God, is he gay? Is that why he never made a move?"

"Yeah. Sure." Gates shrugged. "Let's get you back to campus. Now, Bri."

"Will you stay with me?" she asked, leaning her head against his shoulder.

He closed his eyes and sighed, clearly restraining himself. "Yes."

"You're the best," she told him before blacking out.

Bryna woke up with a headache from hell.

She sat up in bed and felt her stomach roll. "Oh God," she groaned, covering her mouth. She stood up as quickly as she could, tripped over something on the floor, and stumbled into the wall.

"Jesus, Bri," Gates grumbled from where he lay on the floor.

She didn't even respond. She rushed to the bathroom and emptied her stomach. After a few minutes of retching, she stood on uneasy feet, brushed her teeth, and wandered back into the room. She felt like absolute shit.

"What are you doing on the floor?" she groaned. She collapsed back into bed.

"Because I'm a gentleman," he joked. He scooted her over and climbed into bed next to her. "How much of last night do you remember?"

She looked up at him uncertainly. "We went to Posse. I was drinking martinis."

He ran a hand over his eyes and then filled her in on the rest of the night. If she hadn't already been sick, then she was pretty sure she would have been again. Her face paled, and she clutched the comforter in her hands.

"Oh my God," she murmured. "I need to go home and see Jude."

"What about your meeting today?"

She shook her head. "I'll tell them I'm sick. I can't believe I said those things to Jude. I can't believe you talked to him. I can't believe Eric is gay."

"All a rather shocking night," Gates agreed. He looked so concerned about her, but she couldn't even function right now.

"Hey," she said, turning to face him. "Thank you for taking care of me. I know this wasn't easy."

Gates smiled wearily and tucked a lock of her hair behind her ear. "Anything for you, B." His hand lingered a second too long. "Well, let's get you back to L.A. before you do anything else stupid."

After a quick shower and a call to the administration, Bryna and Gates were on their way back to Los Angeles. Bryna tried to reach Jude on the drive, but he didn't pick up. She was disappointed but not surprised. It seemed to be his MO to hole up whenever he was pissed off. She didn't really blame him for being angry this time. She had a good excuse for being in Vegas, which she would explain to him when they finally spoke. She honestly didn't think she needed an excuse for being there with Gates since they were just friends and nothing had happened besides her drunken ridiculousness. However, she did need to apologize for how she had acted on the phone. *What the hell was I thinking?*

She had completely blacked out, so she really didn't even know. Her best guess was, she hadn't been thinking at all.

As soon as Bryna returned from Las Vegas, she hopped in her car and drove over to Jude's apartment. She couldn't let him sit there and obsess over what had happened. If New Year's were any indication, she wouldn't hear from him for over a week…not until he cooled off. But they had too much to discuss to wait that long.

She parked her car and then walked up to his apartment. Her stomach was in knots as she knocked on the front door. When nothing happened, she knocked again.

Still nothing.

She pulled out her phone and tried calling him. The phone went straight to voice mail. *Fuck!* He was ignoring her.

When pounding on the door accomplished nothing, she returned to her car and sat down in horror. She had fucked everything up. All she had wanted to do was experience college the way she was supposed to. She wouldn't have ever been there if it weren't for her dad, and now, her relationship was going up in flames. She choked back on the ache spreading out from her chest. *I cannot lose Jude over this!*

Just as she was about to pull out from the garage, a text came in.

> *Can't talk right now.*

She messaged back.

> *Please let me explain.*

> *I'm not free again for two weeks.*

Bryna checked her calendar and cursed. Of course he would pick her busiest weekend of the year. Gates's premiere and the Pink Charity Benefit.

> *I can meet you late Friday night. It's Valentine's Day.*

> *Fine.*

She ground her teeth. She had so much she wanted to say in that moment.

> *Call me when you can. I would really like to apologize.*

She waited for him to respond, but when he didn't, she pulled out of the parking lot and started driving. She was halfway home when she received his last message.

I can't call. I'm with my wife.

Her heart plummeted.

TWENTY-SEVEN

"GATES, OVER HERE!" a reporter yelled.

"Mr. Hartman, please a word."

"He's so hot!" someone screamed from the crowd.

"A picture, please."

"Right this way!"

Bryna smiled through the blinding white flashes of light. Reporters with camera crew littered the red carpet on Hollywood Boulevard for the *Broken Road* premiere. A crowd had started forming behind the police barricades hours before the stars were expected to show.

Tonight, Gates was the star.

Crowds cheered for him. Women swooned at his smile. Even the reporters weren't immune to his charm. He was all charisma tonight. Completely in his element.

Bryna, on the other hand, had been out of it for the past two weeks of Jude's silence. It was straight up torture. She wanted to find out what the fuck he was doing with his wife, but her heart and stomach twisted because the question was dangerous. It would lead to a road of additional questions she didn't want to ask herself, but she couldn't seem to stop. *Did he lie about being separated? Has he been with his wife the whole time? Were all the times he claimed to be at work really an excuse for him being with* her*? Is that why he couldn't see me? Are they sleeping together? Am I no better than my stepmother after all?*

All that tension left Bryna stressed and erratic. So, she focused her attention on the charity benefit. She dove head first into planning and tomorrow night all her efforts would pay off. If she could get through the benefit, then things would go back to being as perfect as they had been in St. Barts.

That meant being a supportive friend to Gates on his big day. She had gone all out, wearing a stunning blue Alberta Ferretti original paired with flashy patterned Louboutin high heels. Gates was in a classic tuxedo and looked dashing.

"Gates, one picture with your date, please," a female reporter requested.

Gates wrapped an arm around Bryna's waist, and they both smiled for the camera.

The camera crew snapped a few shots.

When they were done, the woman said, "You make a great couple."

Bryna felt her cheeks heat, and she glanced at Gates.

"Thank you," he said.

"Our readers have been asking whether or not you are still taken. Some thought, or maybe were hoping, your relationship was over." The reporter laughed and conspiratorially smiled at Bryna. "We'd love to hear your love story."

"Oh, we're not—" Bryna started to say.

"We prefer to keep our personal life private," Gates said instead.

The reporter switched tactics. "Everyone saw you two together on New Year's. I even heard there was a kiss," she said, raising her eyebrows. "Can you confirm that?"

"We were together for New Year's," Gates acknowledged. "But I don't kiss and tell."

"A gentleman," the reporter acknowledged. "Is it true that you were recently spotted out in Las Vegas together as well?"

Gates nodded. "That's right."

"A budding romance. Can you tell us how you feel about her?"

Bryna kept her fake smile on her face, but she was ready to get out of this situation. Pretending with Gates was fine for the red carpet, but it was enough that her stepmother thought they were still dating. She didn't need the rest of the world to know that as well.

"We already said, we keep our lives private," she said.

"Bri, it's okay if they know," Gates said, squeezing her waist.

She raised her eyebrows at him in confusion. "Know what?"

"How I feel about you," Gates said softly. His eyes stared into her, all bright blue and pleading. He looked like he wanted to tell her something, like he'd been holding it in for a while. "Everyone else seems to know but you anyway."

Bryna's mouth opened slightly in surprise. *He is not doing this right now!*

"Gates, are you saying you love her?" the reporter asked, thrusting the microphone forward. "Care to comment further?"

"No, he does not," Bryna said. She took his hand and marched him down the rest of the red carpet and inside the theater.

Bryna had been here before for her father's premieres, so she quickly found them an empty room. She shoved Gates inside and glared at him.

"What the fuck was that about?" she demanded.

He glared right back at her. "What the fuck do you think it was about, Bri?"

"I came to this premiere with you because we're friends, which I've said to you over and over again. I agreed to go months ago. And you have been so good to me lately that I wanted to do something nice for you, but I'm not your girlfriend!"

"You think I don't know that?" he growled. "You remind me every chance you get. I can't help that I'm in love with you, Bri."

Bryna rolled her eyes. *Is he really playing this game?* "Stop! We're not even in front of the cameras. You don't have to bullshit me and pretend that you're in love!"

Gates's eyes flashed with anger. "Pretend? You think I'm fucking pretending? I do love you, Bri. I have for a long time."

She shook her head. He had no idea what he was saying. It wasn't true. It couldn't be. "No, you don't."

"If I could love someone else, don't you think I would have already done it? You're a psychotic bitch most of the time, and you drive me crazy, but I love you." He threw his hands out and stomped across the room, away from her. "For some unknown fucking reason."

"You're just saying that because I'm with someone else now." God, she hoped that was the case.

"Do you fucking hear yourself? You are out of your goddamn mind. And don't even bring that fucker into this conversation."

"Jude?" she asked.

"Yeah. Fuck that guy!"

"What is wrong with you?"

He looked manic.

Where is this all coming from?

He flung his hands up in the air. "Wrong with *me*? You're the one who thinks you're in love with this guy. He's deluded you with presents and exotic trips, so you think that's fucking love, but he's just using you."

"You don't even know him!" Bryna cried angrily. *How dare he throw all this out at me now!*

"I don't fucking need to. I know how he treats you, and I know what he said to me that night in Vegas. That's all I need to know about this guy to know he's a fucking douche."

"You're being ridiculous."

"See? You don't even want to know the truth. You don't care that he only wants you when it's convenient to have sex with you."

"Fine!" she spat. "What did he say to you?"

Gates laughed contemptuously and looked away from her. "After I told him I'd just be taking you back to the hotel to sleep, he said that if I laid one finger on you, he'd tear me apart limb from limb. That I needed to do the *right thing* and stay away from you…for your own good. He asked if I understood that there would be hell to pay if he found out otherwise."

Bryna paused where she was standing. "He said that?" she asked softly. It sounded really hot…like Jude really wanted her.

"Yes. It's the most unhinged, controlling, douchey thing to say when I was only trying to *help* you."

Should I see that as controlling, or was Jude only looking out for me? "You still stayed the night," she reminded Gates.

He glared at her. "Would you have rather I left you there to drown in your own vomit?"

"No, but Jude was right."

Gates looked at her in utter disbelief, as if he was seeing a completely different person. It was an unsettling stare. "I can't do this, Bryna. I can't do this with you anymore."

She eyed at him uneasily. "What do you mean?"

"What do I mean?" He stared at her like he was seeing her for the first time. "I told you that I loved you, and you act like I'm fucking jealous. I'm the one who has been there for you through all the bullshit, Bri, and you thank me for being there for you, but it's not out of appreciation. It's an expectation. You were flirting with me on New Year's before we kissed. You took me away from a girl I was hitting on at Posse and then joked around about how sex with me sounded fun. The mixed signals have pushed me over the edge. You think because you say we're friends that it'll magically happen. But that's not how it fucking works!"

"I don't know what you want me to say," she whispered taken aback.

"Nothing. It's obviously too much for me to expect you to say anything." He shook his head. "You might think you're queen bee, but I'm not the same person I was when we first met. I'm a movie star. We're at my fucking premiere. I could be doing whatever and whoever the fuck I want."

"Then, do that," Bryna said harshly. "I'm not fucking stopping you."

"Good. Because I'm not fucking around anymore." He brushed past her toward the door and then spoke quietly, facing away from her, "I used to think you were everything, Bri. Now, I realize that you were just a waste of my time. You're not queen. You're just another desperate wannabe. And you're no longer welcome here."

"What?" she snapped. Her mouth dropped open.

He turned around, and his eyes were icy. "Leave. Before I have to alert security."

With that, he walked out the door, leaving Bryna standing alone in the empty room with her hands shaking, her breath coming out in shocked sputters, and her mind reeling.

TWENTY-EIGHT

PINK WAS THE COLOR OF THE EVENING.

Rosé champagne in pink-rimmed flutes. Waitresses in baby-pink sequined skirts, carrying pink trays with pink champagne cupcakes. Ornate shimmering pink crystal chandeliers, pink peony bouquets atop waist-high cocktail tables, and already dozens of women wearing gorgeous designer pink dresses.

Bryna was standing at the entrance table in a tight hot-pink Dior dress with the Harry Winston B necklace on, overseeing the idiots she had gotten to replace Avery and Tara. She had given them the guest list Felicity had made and informed them that they had to know every single person who was attending by face. She didn't want any awkward moments where they would have to ask for a person's name. Clearly, neither of them had done their homework.

"Lauren, are you completely incompetent?" Bryna snapped. "How could you not recognize Jeremiah

Anderson? He's a very important alumnus and successful producer. I know he was on the list!"

"Sorry, Bri." Lauren frantically looked around as if she thought the other assistant, Julie, would help her. "I...I guess I just forgot. He didn't seem to mind—"

"I mind! You should have been more prepared for this." Bryna shook her head in disgust. "You'd better get the next person right."

Felicity flitted over to the table with a big smile on her face. She was practically glowing. It was the happiest Bryna had seen the bitch since they started working together.

"Bryna, everything is going so wonderfully. Thank you for all the hard work you've put in."

"I'm so happy I was able to help, Felicity," Bryna said with a fake smile.

She was shocked she could keep her temper under control, even for this moment.

After her argument with Gates at the premiere, she had left in shock. Part of her had wanted to find the first reporter on the red carpet and let the media know about Gates and Chloe. But she couldn't. As much as she was humiliated by what had happened, she cared about Gates too much to out him to the press.

But she hated that they weren't in a good place, and he wasn't here tonight. She couldn't believe how judgmental he was regarding Jude. It ate at her more than she wanted to admit. Not to mention, she was freaked out about finally getting to see Jude tonight after the benefit. Her stomach was in knots, and it only increased her irritability.

"Oh, look! Our special guests have arrived!" Felicity said.

Bryna turned around to see who was walking in the door, and her mouth dropped. "Daddy?"

"Hey, sweetheart!" her father said, enveloping her in a hug.

"What are you doing here? I thought you were still in New Zealand!"

"We wrapped up this week. I immediately flew home for my little girl's big charity event. Celia told me all about it."

Bryna looked on in surprise. *My father flew all the way from New Zealand to be here for me?* Her eyes shifted to Celia, who smiled politely, and then to the person standing next to her. *Pace.* He stared at her as if he knew all her secrets, and she quickly looked away.

"I'm so glad you're here."

Her father quirked his head to the side. "Now, Celia told me one other thing. Something about a boyfriend? Where is Gates? We need to have a talk."

Bryna's face fell. "Oh, uh…he wasn't able to make it. The *Broken Road* premiere was last night." She hated lying, but telling the truth at this point would be more work.

"Next time then, kiddo." He patted her shoulder and then introduced himself to Felicity.

Pace walked forward and leered at her. "No Gates tonight, huh? Fake boyfriend didn't want to make an appearance?"

"Leave me alone, Pace," she said warningly.

"What about Avery and Tara? No fake friends tonight either?"

"Just go!" she snapped.

He smirked. "Have a good night."

She glared at his back. She wanted to relish in the fact that her father was here and not worry about Pace. He couldn't ruin her night. She had worked too hard for this.

Felicity laughed at something Bryna's father said. He shook her hand and then disappeared into the crowd with Celia.

"Your father is quite the charmer."

"That he is," she agreed.

"Well, keep up the good work. I'm going to entertain the guests. I'll be back to fetch you when your work is done," Felicity said.

Bryna glumly watched her walk away. She wanted to enjoy the party that she had created. She knew that it wasn't unreasonable to have her working the front of the event while so many people were showing up, but mingling sounded like so much more fun.

"Bryna! This man isn't on the list," Lauren said. "I'm sorry, sir. We'll get this all cleared up."

She turned around, and her heart skipped a beat. "Jude?"

His head snapped back. His mouth opened slightly in surprise. His gaze traveled up her legs, over the hot-pink dress, and then to her face. After he soaked her in and seemed to realize that she was real, his eyes darted around the room. "Bri, what are you doing here?"

"This is my event," she said.

Suddenly, her stomach turned to ice. If he was here, at a Harmony event, then he could find out at any second that she wasn't here as an alumnus but as a student.

"What are *you* doing here?" she asked him.

He opened his mouth and then closed it. He didn't seem to know how to answer the question. His inability to give a logical answer only made her that much more fearful.

"Oh, Jude, you're here!" Felicity called from behind her, appearing out of the crowd. "Sorry. I forgot to add you to the guest list."

He stared at Felicity with a tormented look on his face, but she didn't seem to notice. She walked right up to him and wrapped an arm around his waist.

Bryna couldn't tear her eyes away. It was like a train wreck. As much as she wanted to avoid the oncoming crash, she couldn't seem to get out of the way.

"Bryna, this is my husband, Jude."

TWENTY-NINE

NO, NO, NO, NO, NO! This couldn't be happening.

Jude wasn't here. Felicity wasn't his wife. Bryna hadn't been having a raunchy affair with the organizer's husband.

She was going to blink, and this nightmare would disappear.

"*This* is Bryna?" Jude asked. Shock was clear in his voice too.

Oh shit! She had only ever told him that her name was Bri.

"The student who has been working with you on the charity event?"

She closed her eyes again, hoping to make this all go away. *Please work!*

Fuck! It isn't working!

Jude's eyes met Bryna's in disbelief and…horror. She was sure that she mirrored his expression. She wanted to say so much to him in the moment, but what could she say?

Yes, I'm a seventeen-year-old high school student. I've been meaning to tell you.

She didn't think that was going to help anything.

"Yes! Isn't she wonderful? She's done the most amazing job," Felicity said. She smiled brightly at Bryna.

His Adam's apple bobbed in his throat as he swallowed.

Right about now would be a good time for some acting skills to kick in.

"Everything looks…great," Jude said.

Smooth.

"I think so, too," Felicity agreed.

"Thanks," Bryna managed to get out. Her stomach was churning, and she was short on breath. She needed to get out of there, get some air, get her emotions under control. "If you'll excuse me, I'm going to find the restroom."

Without a backward glance at Jude, she turned and walked directly into the crowd.

She was horrified, and surely, everyone would notice. But she pushed through the benefit guests, toward the back of the room, anyway. She couldn't believe what had happened. Tonight was supposed to be the night she and Jude worked out all their issues. They were going to be honest with each other, but she hadn't expected it to ever happen this way!

And the look on his face when he had found out.

She choked down the pain. He'd been disgusted with her. She had thought that when she finally told him that she was still in high school, it wouldn't matter because they would be on equal footing…equally in love.

But how could he look at me like that if he was in love with me? How could he love me if he showed up tonight to be with Felicity?

She just needed a minute to think before panic set in. She rushed into the restroom, and the room was mercifully empty. She locked herself into a stall and leaned her head back against the door as she closed her eyes.

What the hell am I going to do?

She could *not* go back out there with Jude and Felicity.

Yet she couldn't leave. She *wouldn't* leave. This was her event. She had done all the work to get this thing running. She wouldn't be scared off because he was here. She would simply avoid him at all costs.

That's possible. Right?

Her hands stopped shaking, and she straightened. After taking a deep breath, she left the stall and stared at herself in the mirror. She was strong. She was the queen. Later, she would figure out what the fuck was happening with Jude and why he had fucking lied to her.

She left the restroom and walked back toward the waiting room of guests. Halfway to her destination, a hand reached out from an open doorway and pulled her inside by the elbow.

"What the—" she cried.

Then, her back hit against a firm body, and a hand covered her mouth. The door was kicked shut, and she let out a muffled scream.

"Bri," Jude whispered into her ear, silencing her outburst.

She breathed heavily in his embrace. Her body molded to his, and despite everything, she was turned on by his touch. She couldn't help her body's reaction to him. It had been too long since she had seen him, and even before she had gotten to know him, his body had set her off. He was still holding her against him, and she wondered if he was thinking the same thing.

How wrong would it be for him to take me right here with his wife in the other room?

God, I'm sick. She was *not* that person!

He had fucking said they were separated. And she had believed him. She hated that he had lied to her about that, but she hadn't known. Now that she did though, it changed everything. She would not be the girl on the side. No matter how she felt about him.

She wrenched herself out of his grip and faced him. "What the fuck are you doing?"

"We need to talk. Now."

"That is the epitome of bad ideas," she said in frustration. "Your wife is out there! I'm leaving."

She started for the door, but he grabbed her again.

"Not before you tell me the truth!" he said. His eyes, which had been so beautiful and comforting, stared at her with anger and confusion.

"The truth about what?" she snapped. She smacked his hand away from her.

"About you. You're a high school student?"

"You want the truth as if I've lied to you!" she snapped. She couldn't believe this was happening right here, right now. "You never asked if I was in high school, if I went to college, what kind of work I was in. You never asked how old I was! You liked the mystery, remember?"

"I met you in a fucking bar. I shouldn't have had to ask you how old you are!"

"Yes, because no one underage goes to bars," she quipped.

Jude ran a hand back through his hair. "This is fucking ridiculous. Just tell me how old you are."

"How old are *you*?" she asked. Even when he had asked her at point-blank, she still had to deflect the question. *Seventeen. Why is that so fucking hard to say?*

"Thirty-two."

Bryna's mouth hung open slightly. She had known he was older, but she had always told herself that he was probably twenty-seven. Only ten years older than her. Not fifteen. *Christ!*

She opened her mouth and then looked away from him. "Seventeen," she whispered.

"Fuck!" he cried, whirling away from her. His hands were balled into fists, and he looked like he was going to punch his way through the nearest wall. "You're a minor! This cannot be happening. We had sex." His eyes found hers across the room. He was panicking. She could see the desperation in his face. "I took you out of the country."

"Yeah, I was there for all that."

"Don't you understand?" he said, rushing back to her and grabbing her by the shoulders. He shook her softly as if to make the message clearer. "If anyone found out, I would be in a world of trouble—statutory rape, child abduction."

"I'm not a child! And I consented to *everything* you did to me." She looked him up and down.

"It doesn't fucking matter that you consented. If you tell anyone it happened, then I'm ruined." He shook his head. Then, his eyes turned demanding. "Promise that you won't tell anyone."

Bryna glared at him. *Is this what we have come to? Promises for my silence?*

"Why should I stay silent when you obviously don't give a shit about *me?*"

He didn't even blink. "I'll give you anything you want to make this go away," he insisted. "What do you want? Money?"

She stumbled backward a step. Her breathing was shallow. *How could he offer it up so casually?* He hadn't even disagreed with her. Until that moment, she would have argued with Gates until it was her last breath. But Jude had offered her money to stay silent. *Has he really been using me all along?*

Even if he had actually liked her, she had never felt more disgusted. "I never wanted you for your money!"

"Oh?" His hand reached out and traced the B on her necklace.

She smacked his hand away. "You gave this to me as a Christmas present! All I wanted was you," she told him earnestly.

"Did you think you could have me?" he asked. He seemed genuinely surprised. "You knew I was married."

"You said you were separated, you motherfucker!" She smacked him across the face. The sound rang out in the small room. She didn't recoil at the anger brimming in his eyes. She just returned the scathing look.

He grabbed her hand and yanked it hard to his side. "When we first met, I was separated from my wife. But ever since New Year's, she's been trying to get us to work things out. That is why I'm here with her."

"I don't want your excuses. Did you ever tell me the truth when we were together?"

"I told you what you needed to know. You liked what I was providing. You appreciated it. I was happy to give it to you."

"Give what exactly? Your body? Your money? But never your heart," she spat.

"You didn't ask for that," he said casually.

"I shouldn't have had to," she snarled. "Who are you, Jude? Where is the man I was falling for?" She felt her resolve weakening, the pain creeping into her heart, the tears threatening to spill out of her eyes. She couldn't mask the torment, but she refused to cry in front of him. He didn't deserve her tears, her mascara was too damn expensive.

"The man you thought you knew was a dream, Bri. An illusion. I can't be that person for you."

"I see that now," she said. Her voice was steely.

Gates had been right all along. Jude didn't love her. With the time they had spent together, the grand gestures, the gifts, the affection…she had thought that he loved her. But she had just been blinded by the fact that Jude was giving her all the things she wasn't getting anywhere else.

She had thought that because he saw into the depths of her heart and understood her suffering that they were connected. Now, she didn't know if that had all been an act for her benefit.

Did he use the line to get me into bed? Has he been playing a game with me the whole time?

Even that first night when she had gotten into his Jaguar, he had cringed at the thought of a gold digger yet…he had created one.

THE DOOR BURST OPEN, and Jude and Bryna scrambled apart.

"What is going on in here?" Felicity asked.

A shadow appeared behind her, and then Pace materialized.

Oh no! He couldn't know what was going on.

"I was talking to Bryna about the event and how it was such a success. I thought we could offer a bigger donation," Jude answered smoothly.

"Is that right?" Felicity asked. Her eyes fell on Bryna.

She hastily looked away. "Yes. He was talking about making a donation." *Just not to the charity.*

"I'm not sure that sounds like a good enough reason for you to be behind closed doors with a high school student," Felicity said pointedly.

"You're right," Jude agreed. "We should have taken our conversation out to the party. I didn't mean to take up all your time."

He started walking toward Felicity, but she crossed her arms and stared at him with a knowing look on her face. "And how exactly do you two know each other?"

Bryna wasn't touching that one with a ten-foot pole. Jude didn't even look at her, which was probably for the best. If he wanted to get out of this situation, then he could fucking figure it out himself. She was done.

"You introduced us," Jude said, as if reminding Felicity of what had just transpired.

"Please," Felicity said, rolling her eyes. "I'm not an idiot, Jude. Don't treat me like one."

"I think you have the wrong idea—"

"I don't believe that I do. Now, tell me, Jude, exactly how long have you known Ms. Turner?"

"Felicity," he said imploringly.

"Cut the crap, Jude. I just want to know if we're seriously doing this again. You couldn't help yourself, could you?"

"Again?" Bryna asked. Her eyebrows shot up, and she looked at Jude questioningly. *Has the fucker done this sort of thing before?*

"Oh, yes, I'm sure my husband didn't tell you that he has a preference for young blondes…or that you weren't the first," she spat.

"Are you fucking kidding me?" Bryna cried. *That bastard!*

"Bri," he groaned, glancing at her again.

She could see that he wanted her to stay silent, but how could he ask that of her? She wasn't even the first person he had seduced like this.

"You would think that having a law degree would make you realize the possible repercussions of your actions. Instead, you act like the football players you manage."

"Football players?" Bryna asked in confusion.

Then, it hit her.

The number one sports agency in the country. "Jude...Rose. Rose Corp."

Bryna's own father had almost signed with them when he was going to go pro. No wonder Jude had known about the sex clubs and how football players acted and why he was gone all the time in the fall. It explained the clients he'd had at Chateau Marmont on New Year's. He hadn't given her his last name because that name was unbelievably well-known in Los Angeles. He wouldn't have wanted her to be able to look him up.

Jude looked between Felicity and Bryna and seemed to realize there was no out. He was a smooth talker, but he couldn't talk his way out of this one. "How did you figure it out?" he finally asked Felicity.

Felicity stepped forward threateningly. The bitch who had tested Bryna to find out if Bryna was good enough to work for her had returned. "I was informed by another student, who had apparently heard you two speaking about having sex and leaving the country." She narrowed her eyes. "Is that true?"

Bryna didn't wait to hear what Jude had to say. Her eyes moved across the room to Pace still standing in the hallway, overseeing what was going on. She glared at him, and he just smirked. She saw everything he had to say in that one smile.

Game. Set. Match.

Asshole.

"I know things are bad, but can't you at least think about Alex for once?" Felicity asked, drawing Bryna's attention back to the conversation.

"Who is Alex?"

"He's our son," Felicity said.

Bryna's world tilted. *Son.* She couldn't comprehend that word. Jude had a kid. Of course, she had never asked if he had children, but she had never even thought about it. He had used her to escape his life, and she didn't even know why. He had an accomplished beautiful wife, who clearly loved him despite his flaws. They had a child together. The whole thing made her feel sick.

"Didn't mention him either, huh?" Felicity asked with bite in her voice.

"Felicity, I didn't know," Bryna said.

"You're young," she said, her voice filled with disgust. "You'll learn what's yours to play with and what isn't."

Bryna recoiled at the comment. She had known Jude was married but thought he was separated. She had thought they weren't getting back together. Perhaps she had just let him delude her into believing that.

"Don't bring her into this," Jude said. "This is my doing."

"Yes, it is," Felicity said. "And it's yours to fix. You can walk out of here with me right now, promise to come home to be with me and be a father to Alex, and never see her or anyone else ever again, or I'll alert the authorities, and you'll never see your son again."

Bryna gasped. Her hand flew to her mouth.

"Oh, don't act so self-righteous!" she snapped at Bryna. "You knew you were sleeping with a married man. You had to know how this would end."

"Why would you even want to be with him?" Bryna managed to get out.

Felicity ignored her. "Your son is waiting for you at home. Choice is yours, Jude."

Then, she turned around and walked out of the room. Bryna stared after her in shock. Her eyes flitted to Jude, but he wasn't looking at her. She wanted to plead with him not to give in, that she wouldn't agree to testify, that Felicity had no proof. And another part of her wanted to see him pay for what he had done to her.

She still had such strong feelings for him that she vacillated so strongly between the two extremes. To save him or to damn him.

Jude sighed heavily and then made the choice for her. He followed Felicity out of the room. He hadn't even bothered to look at Bryna. He had left her standing there, all alone.

Pace chuckled from the doorway and then disappeared without a word. He hadn't even needed to land a blow. She'd had enough.

No friends. No Gates. No Jude.

Her hands balled into fists at her sides. She took a deep breath and then slowly released it. Ice filled her veins, chilled her blood, hardened her heart.

She would not be sad about Jude. *How could I be when everything I truly knew about him has been shattered in a matter of minutes? How could I be when he walked out without even the decency of saying good-bye?* She was a realist. She had known as soon as Felicity walked through the door that their chance was over.

But grow some fucking balls!

Jude should have owned up to what they had done and told Felicity that he wasn't happy in their marriage. He shouldn't have been a pussy by running back to her with his tail between his legs.

No, Jude had made it clear that he had never been hers. They were just strangers with memories.

She wasn't sad. She was pissed. She wanted to tear everything apart. Destroy it. Burn it to the ground. Just so the world could feel a fraction of what was annihilating her heart.

She had lost *everything* since that first night she had left with Jude. She had abandoned and neglected Avery and Tara and then further isolated them by kicking them off the committee. Part of it had been related to Pace, but she had been so irritated about what was going on with Jude that she wasn't able to think straight.

And Gates. He *loved* her. *What did I do in return?* Taken advantage of him. Made him deal with her Jude-induced insanity. Accused him of being jealous. Pushed him away.

She couldn't rebuild that. *How could he forgive me? How could I even ask him to forgive me?*

She had let her guard down once. Just once for Jude. Now, it had all been thrown right back in her face.

Never again.

She would never again suffer like this. She would take control. She would call the shots. She already had a game plan and knew what she needed to do.

She touched the Harry Winston B at her throat, admiring her scarlet letter. If Jude had wanted to create a gold digger, then a gold digger she would become.

The End

The second book in the
All That Glitters series
is available for preorder
at select retailers.

GOLD

July 7th

GOLD

USA Today Bestselling Author
k.a. linde

so ask yourself if you are willing to burn. because the moment you open yourself to me, i will have no choice but to scorch everything that defines you. and without regret, i will devour and i will leave nothing behind.

—r.m. drake

ONE

HELL HATH NO FURY like a woman scorned.

That was the damn truth.

Bryna twirled her Harry Winston B diamond necklace around her finger and parted her pouty lips. She had decided on a gold glitter Chanel dress and hot-as-fuck Jimmy Choos, and when she walked into Las Vegas State's local nightclub, Posse, all eyes turned her way. Just the way she liked it.

She was still getting used to her new life in college. No annoying cling-ons. No obnoxious stepbrother. No wannabe stepmother. No reminders of what happened her senior year when her life was shot to hell. No reminders of *him*.

Just her scarlet letter hanging around her neck and a new crowd to rule.

This was the life.

"Bryna! Over here!" Trihn called from the bar.

Bryna fluttered her fingers at her friend and walked her way. It was strange, in a way, to have friends. In high school, she had always had Gates Hartman, her movie star ex-boyfriend, but that had crashed and burned. Otherwise she usually considered other girls as either followers or competition. With Trihn, there was none of that.

Trihnity Hamilton may be model tall and exotic with endless brown-to-blonde ombre hair, but she was the nicest, most sure-of-herself person Bryna had ever met. They had met in this very club the first week of school. Trihn had confidently commented on Bryna's next season Christian Louboutins. After a night of shots and dancing, a friendship had blossomed.

"Look at you rocking the Chanel tonight after the big game," Trihn said. She pulled Bryna in for a hug. "I think glitter is your color."

Bryna laughed. "Always. Look at you in your rocker grunge."

"Excuse me. This is designer rocker grunge," Trihn corrected her.

She wore skin-tight black leather pants, a ripped white crop, and strappy Gucci high heels she had probably gotten when she modeled for them last year. Bryna was constantly surprised that they got along and Trihn had a real personality. She normally thought model types were dumb as bricks.

"Ahhhh!" a girl screamed, barreling into Bryna. "You look fucking hot!"

"I'm surprised you're not still in uniform," Bryna said.

Stacia Palmer was on the cheerleading team with Bryna. Her father was the head football coach at their biggest rival, the University of Southern California, and that would have made her the enemy, but she had come to LV State to stay out of her father's shadow. It also explained her obsession with football players. Her reputation as a jersey-chasing whore really endeared her to Bryna. She appreciated the honesty.

"Oh, please." Stacia flipped her bleached blonde bangs out of her eyes. "All the guys here know I'm a cheerleader. Plus, Blaine isn't even here yet. I just made a circuit to see if I could find him."

Blaine was the starting quarterback of the Gamblers football team. Stacia was determined to hook-up with him. Though her real goal was to marry an NFL quarterback.

"You're ridiculous. How can you even stand college guys?" Bryna asked.

"Don't talk to me about older guys. Blaine is a senior, Bri. That's good enough for me."

Bryna arched an eyebrow. "Whatever you're into."

"Like Eric." Stacia sighed heavily. "I would be very into him if he was still playing."

Bryna's eyes wandered through the crowd of football players to where Eric Wilkins was standing. She *had* been very into him on her school visit here last semester, still was sometimes when she forgot the reason that they would never hook up. She was pretty sure that none of her friends and certainly no one on the football team actually knew the reason.

Eric was gay. That was why he had never tried to hook up with her on her visit and why he hadn't talked to her since.

"I don't think you're his type," Bryna said.

"Whatever. I heard the guys talking about how he dated that psychotic head case last year. What was her name?"

Bryna raised her eyebrows. She hadn't heard anything about this. Must have been one hell of a cover story.

"Audrey," Trihn said.

"That's it."

"Why did they break up?" Bryna asked.

Stacia shrugged. "Who cares? She was a crazy bitch. But now he's on the market. So, we can all take our chance with him. What do you say, B?"

She laughed again and shook her head. "I don't think *I'm* his type either."

"Bri...you're everyone's type," Trihn said.

"I appreciate the sentiment."

Normally, she wouldn't disagree with Trihn. She had perfect long blonde hair, a very impressive rack, and a killer body to boot. Most guys couldn't tear their eyes from her, and she had always enjoyed the attention. After the disaster of a senior year, she had especially enjoyed that attention this summer lying on various European beaches and hooking up with gorgeous exotic men who she couldn't understand.

"So, then just go ask him out." Trihn nudged her.

Stacia started cracking up. "Ask him out! You want Bryna to ask him out?"

Bryna rolled her eyes. "You know that's not happening. Do you know who I am?"

"The elusive Bryna Turner," Trihn said with a wink. "Come on. You should be confident enough to be able to ask him out. I'd do it."

"You do it then and let him turn you down. I'm not interested."

"Well, *I'm* interested," Stacia said.

The girls didn't get it. Bryna had never considered herself a good person. In fact, she normally figured she was a class A bitch. But she wasn't about to tell people that Eric was gay. He obviously wasn't out, and the last thing she wanted was for it get back that she was the one who had outed him. She admired him too much to spew venom.

After all, he had led LV State to a national championship as a defensive back before he completely blew out his knee, ending his career. Now he was a student assistant coach for the team, which meant they always hung in the same circles. So, for now, she kept her mouth shut and tolerated her friend's ridiculous behavior.

"You know what," Bryna said with a smile. A plan was already formulating in her mind. "I'll go ask him out."

"Yes!" Trihn cried, thinking she had won.

"But…when he's not interested I get a big fat I-told-you-so, and you bitches find guys to buy us the next round of shots."

"Easy for us," Trihn said. "There's no way he's not interested."

Bryna smirked. *This is almost too easy.*

She honed in on Eric. He was easy to spot even in the crowd of football players. Tall and still built like he played ball with short-cropped dark hair and an easy smile. The guys he was hanging out with had a bunch of girls desperately clinging to them, but Eric was unsurprisingly without one. He may be telling everyone else that it was because of his psycho ex, but she knew the truth. They always said all the hot ones were gay.

"Hey, Eric," Bryna said, interrupting their conversation. "Can I talk with you a minute?"

She felt the eyes of all the other football players heating her skin, but she kept her focus on Eric. She wet her lips and looked up at him under her long lashes. One of the other guys murmured something vulgar under his breath, and Eric shoved him.

"Sure, Bryna. What's up?" he asked nonchalantly.

Bryna pointed her French manicured finger to a more private location. "Mind if we talk over there?"

He nodded and then followed her away. The guys immediately started cat calling him. He flipped them off, returning his attention to her. "What's going on?"

When she stared up into his honey hazel eyes, her smile widened. *God, he is fucking hot.* She had always thought so. Too fucking bad.

"Bryna?"

She snapped out of her trance and remembered why the fuck she was here in the first place. "Do you want to go out sometime?"

Eric stared back at her blankly. He looked surprised, but underneath the shock was something else. She couldn't quite put her finger on it.

"You're asking me out?"

"I know shocker, right?" She tried to play it off as if it wasn't a big deal. She had never really done this before. Mostly because she didn't need to. She was hot and guys flocked to her. This was just to prove a point.

"Look, I…I don't think you're my type." He scratched the back of his head awkwardly. "Nothing against girls like you, but they're just not for me."

Bryna's mouth fell open. "Girls like me?"

"You know what I mean." His eyes fell to the floor.

There it was in his voice again. Was that...*disgust* she detected?

"No, I don't think I do. I've been here less than a month. What exactly is my reputation that you can say 'girls like me'?"

Eric sighed and his eyes found her once more. "You know what people say about you...about all the cheerleaders," he clarified quickly. "No offense. I'm just not into that."

"Them now and not just me."

She didn't even know why she was taking offense to all this. She had been expecting him to turn her down. She had expected him to say no that he didn't want to go out with her. But she sure as hell hadn't expected him to basically call her a slut bag whore. People like *her*! *What the hell did that even mean?*

She hadn't even slept with anyone here! Three weeks at Las Vegas State, and while she had played the field, she was wary of getting too close to anyone. The last thing she wanted was for feelings to get involved and fuck her up again. All she wanted was some hot meaningless sex. And it was harder to come by from someone who went to her school knowing they would inevitably run into each other.

"I don't want to get into it, Bryna. But it's...cute that you asked me."

Cute.

He had said it was *cute*. This had gone from irritating to humiliating with one word. What an asshole!

"Maybe call up your friend, Gates. He seemed into you."

"We're not friends anymore, but thanks," she spat sarcastically.

Bryna turned to walk away, but Eric reached out and grabbed her arm. "Hey. I didn't mean to offend you. I didn't know you two weren't friends anymore."

"Let me go," she growled.

Eric immediately dropped her arm. He had that look again like he was already disgusted with her, and her harsh tone only made it worse. "Whatever."

Bryna stormed away back to her friends. She struggled to find composure. The thought of Gates irritated her to no end. He had been in love with her, and everything had gone straight to shit. She hadn't even talked to him since he had kicked her out of his movie premiere, and now Eric Wilkins was bringing it up.

Ugh! Just another reminder of that night. Another reminder of what she had lost. Another reminder that she had let *him* get to her. Another reminder of how fucking pissed off she was at what *he* had done.

She took a deep breath and shut down. She locked away the image of *him*. She swallowed hard. This wasn't right. His name held no power over her. Never again would he hold any power over her.

Jude.

She locked away the image of Jude, the man she had once loved, telling her he was married with a son. Locked away the memory of him turning around, following his wife out of the banquet room, and leaving her forever.

She shouldn't let this get to her. Gates was out of her life. Jude was out of her life. And Eric Wilkins didn't matter.

ACKNOWLEDGMENTS

THE ALL THAT GLITTERS SERIES has been in my head for several years, and I'm so glad that I was finally able to write Bryna and the start to her crazy world. This book would not have been completed without many other people helping me!

First, I'd like to thank the random hostess at the Mexican restaurant three years ago, who gave the absolute best service my sister and I ever had. She had a really freaking cool name, too, that I'd never heard before. I wasn't sure how to pronounce it, and she told me it was pronounced *Brihn-uh*. So, I'm not sure if she'll appreciate that I immortalized her name as a slightly manic gold digger, but thanks anyway!

Second, to the group of girls who read this book while I wrote it, gave me feedback, and generally kept me from going crazy! Jessica—thank you for loving the assholes I create, no matter what villainous things they do. Bridget—thank you, in turn, for always loving my nice guys and inevitably making me want to write books about them. Rebecca—thank you for good music and seemingly sharing a brain with me. And, of course, thank you to Diana Peterfreund, who whipped my ass into shape and gave me invaluable advice while writing. ♥

Also, to my early readers—I really appreciate you taking a chance on Bri and your expert feedback. I know she's kind of a lovable unlikable character, but she just kind of owns it. So, thank you, Trish Brinkley, Katie Miller, Lori Francis, Jessica Sotelo, and Amy McAvoy.

Ahhhh! Lauren Blakely, thank you so much for the incredible blurb for this book as well as for taking a chance on my angst-filled ride. P.S. Can we go to Paris? I need some new jeans. Also, thank you to Emma Hart, Kendall Ryan, and Corinne Michaels, who let me drive them crazy during the months before this book released.

I'd like to thank Sarah Hansen of Okay Creations, who created this brilliant masterpiece of covers for the All That Glitters series. I basically handed you the titles, and you completely blew me out of the water!

As always, thank you to my beautiful editor and formatter, Jovana Shirley at Unforeseen Editing! You always do a fantastic job on all your books, and this one is no exception.

Additionally, thank you to Christine at Shh Mom's Reading, for dedicating so much time to putting together all my release information and generally keeping me on task!

I'd also like to thank my family, who encouraged me to write this book when the idea to write a how-Bryna-became-a-gold-digger book popped into my mind on the seven-hour drive to New Orleans for our cruise. Thanks for dealing with my randomness when I'd get up at three a.m. on the ship, pull out my laptop, and just start typing away because I couldn't get Bryna out of my head. Couldn't be here without you. Love you Mom, Dad, Brittany, and Shea. And, of course, I couldn't get through everyday life without my fiancé, Joel, and my two puppies, Riker and Lucy. ♥

Last, but certainly not least, YOU! I want to thank you for taking a chance and reading the first in this new series I'm already wildly obsessed with. Thank you for purchasing this book, for hopefully loving it, and for writing me a short review on what you thought! I can't wait for you to get the second book in the series, *Gold*! Love you all! And thank you for letting me pursue my dreams!

ABOUT THE AUTHOR

USA TODAY BESTSELLING AUTHOR K.A. LINDE has written the Avoiding series, the Record series, and the Take Me series as well as her new adult stand-alone *Following Me.* This is the first in her four-book All That Glitters series.

She grew up as a military brat traveling the United States and Australia. While studying political science and philosophy at the University of Georgia, she founded the Georgia Dance Team, which she still coaches. Post-graduation, she served as the campus campaign director for the 2012 presidential campaign at the University of North Carolina at Chapel Hill.

An avid traveler, reader, and bargain hunter, K.A. lives in Athens, Georgia, with her fiancé, Joel, and two puppies, Riker and Lucy.

K.A. Linde loves to hear from her readers! Feel free to contact her here:

kalinde45@gmail.com
www.kalinde.com
www.facebook.com/authorkalinde
http://twitter.com/AuthorKALinde

CPSIA information can be obtained
at www.ICGtesting.com
Printed in the USA
LVOW12s1711190117
521537LV00003B/571/P